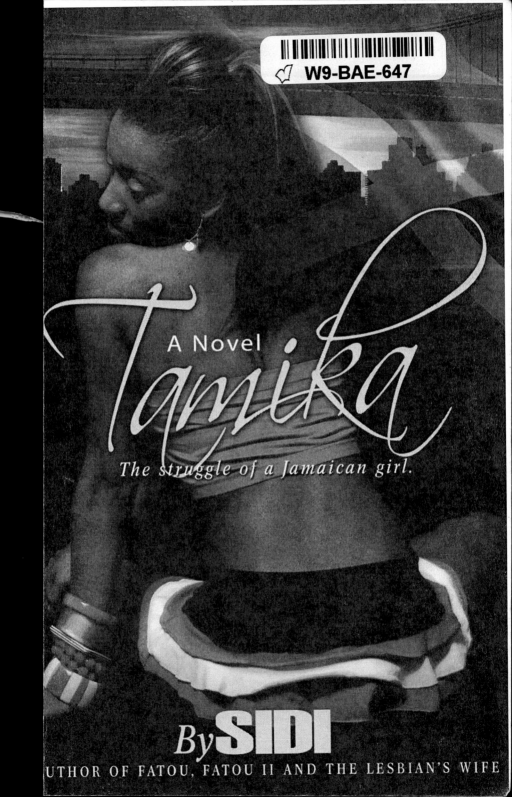

A Novel

Tamika

The struggle of a Jamaican girl.

By SIDI

UTHOR OF FATOU, FATOU II AND THE LESBIAN'S WIFE

Published by:

Harlem Book Center, Inc.
106 West 137th Street, Suite 5D
New York, NY 10030
Phone: 212.316.1213 / 646.739.6429
info@harlembookcenter.com
www.harlembookcenter.com

Warning!
This is work of fiction. All the characters, incidents and dialogues are the products of the author's imagination and are not to be construed as real. Any references or similarities to actual events, entities, real people, living or dead, or to real locales are intended to give the novel a sense of reality. Any similarity in other names, characters, entities, places and incidents is purely coincidental.

Cover Design/Graphics: www.mariondesigns.com
Editor: Barbara Colasuonno

© Copyright 2006
ISBN 0-9763939-1-3

ACKNOWLEDGEMENTS

First of all, I'd like to thank Allah for allowing me to complete this project. To my beautiful family, thanks for being patient with me while my mind was concentrating on getting this novel done.

I am truly thankful to Roland T Books vendor (Brooklyn Mall) for pushing me into a journey of writing books.

To my people running the book business in the streets, Omar Traore "Rubbish" from 125th Street, Tony Brown, Balde, Ishmael Sangnan, Massamba Amar Jamaica (Queens), Mustapha, Konate Moriba "le Gouru", Yigo Aboubacar, Abdou Boussou, Abo Ndiaye, 23th Street, 6 Ave, Cheikhona Ba, 44th Street, Lex. And a special thanks to the two beautiful models, Sidibe Ibrahime "Papito" and Maimouna Ouedraogo "Mai La Princesse".

Special thanks to: J P Morgan Chase Bank-Harlem, Branch 61, Sean Burrows, Sarah, Jacinth Fairweather, Sharyn Peterson, Sharon Font, Sonya Merriel and Bonita Veal.

To my brother-in-law, Fadiga Aboubacar, Sidibe Hadja, Amy, Sidibe Zenab, and Aicha (Ohio) thanks for supporting and believing in me.

Special thanks to my friend, Hubert Daleba Gnolou. I know you been always there for me.

To my best friend, Meite Ibrahim Jean. Thank you for holding me down.

To my friends James W. Martin Jr. aka Jalike Ashanti Heru Herukhati, and Norma van Demark aka Ewunike Adesimbo.

Thanks to A & B and Culture Plus for their support and for believing in me.

To my partner Bakary Gasama (B.K), thank you for your support and encouragement.

Thanks to all of the readers who sampled the manuscript and gave me their feedback. There are too many of you to name individually, but you all know who you are, and I'm extremely grateful.

To my special friends from Sweden, Lisa Eriksson and and Haddy Sarr.

To my family Carlson (Bo, Inger, Jeanette and Angelica). Thank you for believing in me and stay up.

To one of my dearest brothers & friend, Sidibe Siaka, his wife, and two sons. I can't thank you enough for what you have done for me.

To my big brother, Ousmane Fofana "Restaurant bon appetit". Thank you for believing in me.

To my friend Marlon L. 162+ Jamaica do your thing.

To my friend from Burundi, Aimable Rulinda.

To Christine Jordan "28 Precinct Harlem". Thank you for keeping our community safe.

To Hakim bookstore, phone: 267-278-7888. I thank you for being there for me.

To my brother, Inza Sangare "Brikiki", and Kashan Robinson, best-selling author, of Veil of Friendship. Thank you so much for your support.

To my friends in Germany. Thank you so much for your support.

To my brother-in-law, Graig, and his beautiful wife, Corinne. Thank you for encouraging me.

To my man from Paris, Aaron Barrer, "le Congolais blanc". Grand merci. To my best friend, Ahmed Kaba "Bajo" le prince charmant de New York". Keep doing your thing.

To my bodyguard, Big Tony, and his family, and to many friends who helped. I cannot name you all but you know who you are. I do love, appreciate and thank you.

To my friend and partner, Raphael, aka Pepe, Trazar Variety Book Store, 40 Hoyt Street, Brooklyn, NY. Thank you for your support.

A special thanks to "PRETTY LETHAL BOOK CLUB" (Lethal, Pretty and Ayesha) Connecticut and New York.

A very special thanks to Black and Nobel (Marketing,Distribution,wholesale and retail.1411W Erie Ave., Philadelphia, Pa.19141. Phone: 215-965-1559. www.blackandnobel.com).

To Lester R. You're a true soldier. Thanks for showing me honesty, determination and desire to achieve. Keep making sense out of the senseless.

To Lester Marrow (Streets of Harlem), the king of urban lit, keep doing your thing.

Finally, I want to thank Barbara Colasuonno, a gentle genius of an editor, whose patience with me will surely serve her well in the other profession she came to as she helped me to write this book.

And a special thanks to Kevin E. Young. If it weren't for you, the project would not have been completed.

Tamika

The Struggle
of a Jamaican Girl

By

Sidi

DEDICATION

I dedicate this book to

Jaqueline Carleson,

Sidibe Mamadi

and

Sidibe Mabana Hillary.

I truly love you.

FORWARD

By an anonymous child molestation survivor

Dear Reader,

I am a victim of the same ordeal that's discussed in this story. I was very self-destructive before reaching the place in my life where I am today. I attempted suicide, chose negative environments, solicitied drugs and engaged in underage sexual behavior.

I had a baby at sixteen. But everything I did wasn't an outcome of that particular event in my life. Rather, the neglect and lack of communication between me and my mother led to my bad behavior.

When I used to look at myself in the mirror, I would think *Your life is not worth living so there's no need for you to exist.* So I used pills and knives to try to erase myself from the planet. But obviously they didn't work.

Then I began drinking and hanging with older crowds. I became an exotic dancer and started selling drugs. I didn't care about myself, and because older men liked my appearance and youth, I used both to my advantage.

I knew I wasn't getting over. I was just covering up for the things I felt inside. I convinced myself that I wasn't worth preserving, educating or even loving. So I ignored all my basic human needs and convinced myself that I was a waste of space.

I never disclosed this information verbally to my mother. But my actions were disrespectful, non-communicative and disconnected. When my mother finally noticed my behavior, she didn't ask me why. She just talked down to me in front of others. Eventually, our animosity turned physical and we fought. The result was that I ran away and got arrested.

I struggled every day with the fact that I was a teenage mom, not believing I was worthy of being someone's mother. My son loved me even if I didn't love myself. But I had sentenced my life to disaster before I even began to live it.

My mother would never have believed the attack that caused so much of my negative behavior. She put too much trust in her "man" and when I told her of his actions, she didn't believe me. That's what hurt me the most.

I didn't like my mother's boyfriend. She was so stuck on him—and the idea of having a man around—that she denied his abuse of me. And my disrespectful behavior towards her pretty much sealed the deal.

She didn't want to believe he could do wrong. He used to

his advantage the fact that my mother and I weren't getting along and accused me of lying. She took his word over mine. Afterwards, I felt even more neglected, inferior and angry. And to add injury to insult, he stayed in my mother's life and I had to deal with him until the day came when she realized who he really was.

Don't think that every man or woman that enters your life is for the better. And don't think your child is up to no good simply because they may be going through an adolescent phase. Investigate who bring around your children. It might prevent a lot of drama and pain.

My mother and I are getting along better now that I'm twenty-two but it took us a long time to get here. I love her but even my love increased the tension between us. We went into therapy together for a couple years. I still go alone twice a year to help me maintain the positive self image I finally achieved.

Now I help counsel teenage girls with my grandmother and have plans to become a hypnotherapist. Helping teens sort out some of the confusion in their lives is my goal.

My advice is to talk to your children as much as possible, even if they seem a little distant. So much can happen when you don't pay attention to them. Watch their behavior patterns. If they change drastically for the worse, something could be very wrong.

If through my experiences I can open eyes, draw attention

to the relationship between parent and child, and help bring closure to their issues, I will be satisfied in knowing that I didn't suffer for no reason.

Sincerely,
Ms. Anonymous

PROLOGUE

"Cappy, no!" I screamed. I pushed and squirmed, but my little body was no match for the six foot five inch frame that was pinning me down.

"You'll get in a lot of trouble for this, Cappy! They aren't kind to ex-cops and pedophiles in prison. Cappy, nooooooooooo!"

Tears streamed down my face. Snot leaked out of my nose. My breathing was very deliberate like I was about to have a panic attack. But none of that mattered to Cappy.

"Cappy, please. Nooooooooooooooooooooo!" I screamed again.

I reached up and scratched his face as deeply as I could.

"You little bitch!" Cappy snapped as he backhanded me across my cheek. It felt like he was peeling my skin off.

"Lay the hell down and relax, you little whore! It'll be fun. Just chill. You'll be loving it by the time it's over."

Cappy leaned down and started nibbling on my ear and kissing on my neck.

"Besides, haven't I been good to you? Haven't I been taking good care of you since your dad's been gone?"

Save for my whimpering and sniffling, I didn't utter a sound. But Cappy wasn't moved. He continued his little speech as if he could break me down. But that was something he could never do.

"I deserve this little reward, Tamika. I deserve it."

With that, he forced his man-sized penis into my child-sized virginal walls. I felt pain, like I was being pricked by hundreds of hot safety pins after they were sterilized with a match.

But splinters weren't removed from my vagina that day, just my virginity. Blood splattered the sheets and my tears drenched the pillow. Between my blood and tears, I was probably dehydrated that day. But I was too young to know. I was too young to know.

The only other time I cried as much as I did then was the day I finally stopped Cappy's abuse. Yet I'm unsure why I cried. He didn't deserve a single tear.

That day, Cappy had come home and immediately started pitching a bitch about how dirty the house was. My mom had gone to the store to buy laundry detergent and the clothes she had been sorting were strewn all over the kitchen floor.

"Where's your mom?" he barked. I don't know why he thought I'd answer. I never spoke to him, ever, after he'd started abusing me.

"You are such a smart-ass little bitch! I work my ass off taking care of this household and this is the thanks I get?"

I rolled my eyes. Truth be told, even though my dad was arrested for being a kingpin, my mom got a thousand dollars a month from him. He set up an account just in case he ever got locked up. He wanted to make sure that there was enough money to take care of me until I turned nineteen.

"Then," Dad used to say jokingly, "You're on you own." Well, I was already on my own even though I wasn't yet nineteen. I already had to be as smart as any adult.

When Cappy took off his gun belt and uniform and draped them across the chair, I set my expression to show him that I wasn't going to fight back that day.

"Why don't you let me get a little bit while I'm on my lunch? I always love a nooner."

I didn't comment.

"Let's go the bedroom, though," he said. "I don't want the neighbors getting nosy. They would never understand our love."

I almost puked, but I followed him up the stairs to my mother's bedroom anyway.

I followed him into the room and when he was completely naked, I backed away.

"I gotta pee," I said and slyly walked out the room.

"Fuck, Tamika!" he yelled after me. "Hurry up!"

Trust me. I am hurrying, I remember thinking.

That day, the upstairs toilet was not working well and Cappy knew I'd have to run downstairs and use the one near the kitchen instead.

I rushed past the bathroom and ran into the kitchen. I tried to be as quiet as possible but I was crying so hard that it was difficult to stop myself from sniffling. I didn't want Cappy to know I was crying.

I grabbed the gun from his belt, making sure to remove the safety. Then I headed back upstairs to my destiny.

This is one nigga who's gonna get what he deserves.

BOOK ONE

My Early Years

CHAPTER ONE

Upside Down

Age 9

I loved my dad. We did everything together. With his Kingston, Jamaican accent, ripped abs, bulging muscles, chocolate complexion, side-splitting sense of humor, and confidence, I just adored him. I wanted my future husband be just like him.

Yet as crazy as I was about my dad, my mom acted like she was twice as crazy about him. So much so that Dad often told her to stop acting jealous of me.

We went to basketball and football games, fishing, skating, bowling. We pretty much did some of everything.

And my dad was the only thug I'd ever heard of who took the time to figure out how to do his daughter's hair. Yes, he struggled through it every time, but he never sent me away when he got frustrated with my wet mop. He took pride in being there for me in every way, making sure my hair always looked pretty —braids, berets, everything.

It could have been embarrassing. But my adoration of him far surpassed any embarrassment I might have felt. I mean, what little girl shops with her dad for her first training bra? Well, I did. And he was as hands-on in the process as any mother would have been.

"Nah, Ma. Her nipples are still showing through material," he had snapped to the salesperson, "She's gonna need something a lot thicker to cover them up for real."

All I could do was put my head down and wish that I could crawl under a rock. He sounded so ghetto. It was embarrassing as hell. But he was there, and for that I was grateful. I felt so much better off than most of the girls in my neighborhood.

I can't tell you how many of the girls in my neighborhood grew up without fathers. They would skip town as soon as they found out they had gotten their women pregnant. They wanted no part of the responsibility. But my dad, he was down for me in every way possible. He'd always been my rock, for real.

Dad didn't know that I knew, but he was planning a big surprise party for my tenth birthday. He wanted me to celebrate it in style. Of course he didn't tell me about it. But come on now! He dragged me all over the place—linen stores, event planners, caterers. What business did my dad have in those places if something real serious wasn't about to go down?

The last place we went was the worst. Not because of where we were going but because of what happened when we were going there.

We were on the Brooklyn Queens Expressway, leaving Harlem and heading to a shop in Queens. All of a sudden, I saw flashing blue lights behind us.

When I turned around, there was a cop car behind us. My dad swore and pulled the car over.

"Don't worry, Tamika," he said. "All my shit is right so we won't get sweated too hard by these Jakes."

I immediately relaxed. Everything my dad told me was the law. So if Dad said it was OK, then it would be OK. Or so I thought.

"Can I see your license and registration?" said the officer that I later learned was named Cappy.

"I guess so," my dad said sarcastically. "But first, can you tell me why you stopped me? I'm going thirty-five in a thirty-five mile an hour zone, so I'm not speeding. It's light outside so you can't say a headlight's not working. I don't have any warrants…"

"Enough," Cappy spat out like he was large and in charge. "I'm the one asking the questions here. You don't need to be saying anything unless I ask you to."

"Whatever," my dad said, handing Cappy his documents.

"Just make this fast. I'm taking my daughter somewhere, and we don't have all day."

"We'll see about that," Cappy said as he walked away.

We sat fidgeting in our seats without talking. I could tell that my dad was irked. That was the only time he didn't talk me to death or clown around with me.

The funny thing, though, now that I think about it, is that the cops were always stopping me and my dad for something. I guess there's something to that profiling thing everyone talks about. I guess they see a black male in a nice ride and assume he's up to something.

And yes, my dad was usually up to something. But the cops didn't know that. I think they just wanted to keep a black man down.

"Excuse me, sir, can you step out of the car?" Cappy asked when he returned to us.

"Excuse me?" my dad snapped back, heated.

"It appears that this car has been reported stolen, sir. You're gonna have to come with me."

"Man, you're crazy out your goddamned mind! This is my fucking car, yo. What type of shit is you on?"

"Sir, we can do this the easy way or the hard way," Cappy said. "This vehicle is coming up as stolen so you're gonna have to come with me. If there's some misunderstanding, it will be dealt with downtown. But for now, you have to come with me."

"This is bullshit!" my dad barked. "I ain't going nowhere until I call my attorney."

"You can call him when we get downtown," Cappy snapped back.

My dad ignored him. He closed the window, picked up his phone and dialed.

"Hello. This is Marley St. Jacques. I need to speak to Mr. Luigi. It's an emergency. OK, I'll hold briefly but you have to hurry up. Some cop is standing outside my car right now."

Dad waited a second.

"Mr. Luigi, can you meet me at the police station? I haven't been arrested yet but this cop is tripping, saying I have to go with him. He's saying that my car is stolen. What's that? Oh, we're on the BQE just leaving Harlem. Just come to the precinct closest to here. If they take me somewhere else, I'll call you back."

My dad ended the call and handed me his cell phone.

"Hit redial and let Mr. Luigi's office know what's going on. I gotta deal with this bullshit."

After he finished instructing to me, he opened his door and started to get out.

"You're a fucking smart ass, aren't you?" Cappy said while grabbing my dad and placing handcuffs on him.

"What about my daughter?" my dad asked. "She's a child! I just can't leave her here."

"She'll come with us and if a relative can't come to the

station, social services will take her until one does."

"My daughter ain't going to no fucking social services!" my dad snapped at Cappy before hollering back at me while being placed in the cop car. "Call your mom, too, Tamika, so she can pick you up. And don't worry about me. I'll be fine. This is some bullshit and trust me, Luigi's gonna deal with it."

After securing my dad, Cappy walked back to the car and addressed me.

"You have to get out the car, too, little girl. It's about to be towed. You're gonna ride in the car with my partner."

Almost on cue, a big, nasty, monstrous looking bear of a man with sergeant stripes on his shoulder appeared.

"Come on with me, Shorty," he said licking his lips.

I had no choice, so I went with him. I sat in his squad car and prayed that everything would be alright with my dad. Little did I know, though, that my whole world was about to be turned upside down.

CHAPTER TWO

Daddy's Gone

Age 10

It had been almost two weeks and my dad wasn't home yet. I was beyond worried.

My mom was rushing me to finish getting ready. She said we were going to my aunt's house, but I knew she was trying to play me. We were undoubtedly about to head to my surprise party.

"Tamika! I'm not gonna tell you again to hurry the hell up," my mom yelled. "We gotta get outta here."

"Yes, ma'am."

I tried to pick up the pace a little. I didn't want to go to my party without my dad.

Just as I was almost done tying my sneakers, I heard the doorbell ring.

"Tamika, get the door!" my mom yelled. "And I hope

your ass is done when you go get it."

"I'm finished, mom," I said as I ran down the stairs. Maybe my dad was playing with me by ringing the bell. I was so excited. But nothing could have ruined my good mood more than who I saw when I opened the door.

Cappy's black ass was standing there in plain clothes looking like Shabba Ranks after a bad accident.

What the hell does he want? I thought when I saw him. I almost closed the door in his face.

"Mom! That cop who locked Daddy up is at the door," I said as rudely as I possibly could. And then I did close the door.

"What the fuck now?" Mom said, irritated. I heard her high heels clopping down the stairs.

When she opened the door, Cappy started talking to her. I couldn't hear what they were saying because they were whispering. I snuck up closer to my mom so I could hear but she spun around and spoke to me in a way I never heard before.

"Girl, get the hell outta my face when I'm talking to somebody! I hate when your ass is all up in my business!"

I was shocked. I slowly retreated to the kitchen, praying that whatever Cappy wanted didn't take long. He was like a bad luck charm to me, like a dark black cloud hovering over me. With him around, nothing good would happen.

After a few minutes, I heard the door close and my mom came into the kitchen.

"Tamika, something just came up. You're gonna have to catch a cab to your aunt's house." She handed me twenty dollars. "You know how to flag down a gypsy cab, right?"

"Awe, Mom. I gotta catch a cab? I want to go with you!"

"Well you don't get everything you want, child! I told you something's come up."

"Dag! I can't stand him!"

"Child, what the hell are you talking about?"

"That cop. He shows up and I know something bad's gonna happen. He gets on my nerves."

"Child, just go to your aunt's and enjoy the rest of your birthday. You and me, we can go shopping later."

"Mom, please!"

"Don't get on *my* damned nerves! I have to do something." She grabbed me and gave me a hug and kiss. "Have a good time and try not to do anything that upsets your aunt. Lord knows she's bipolar."

"OK, Mom. I love you," I said as she walked away. "But I wish you were going with me," I mumbled under my breath.

When I opened the door at my Aunt Toni's on 158th and Amsterdam everyone yelled "Surprise!"

I pretended to be for their benefit but I was far from surprised. What did surprise me was how phat the apartment looked.

There had to have been at least two hundred balloons, and flowers were everywhere. There was a fountain with an ice statue of me. Who in the hood ever had an ice statue? That was my dad. Going all out for his baby and not even around to see the result.

I tried to be strong but eventually I started to cry.

"Awe," my cousins swooned.

"She's all shook up," my cousin Sabrina chimed in. "I would be crying too, girl, if my dad did all this for me. But I can barely get him to come get me for the weekend or give me five dollars to go skating."

"Yeah, her dad is good as hell to his daughter," Aunt Toni added. "No one would ever say that he doesn't love his daughter. But what's taking your mom so long to park the car?"

"She's not parking the car, Aunt Toni," I said unenthusiastically. "She's not coming. She gave me twenty dollars for cab fare here and back."

"What?! What do you mean she's not coming?" she snapped, irritated. "She's your mother. She's required to come to your birthday party!"

"Well, she said something came up. I begged her but she said no. It must be something real important." I was getting annoyed at my aunt for making me defend my mother when I was so angry at her myself. "You know how my mom gets when her mind's made up about something."

"Umm, umm, umm. Katrina gets on my damned nerves," Aunt Toni said. "Ain't nothing in the world gonna come up that would stop me from celebrating my daughter's birthday with her. And your dad's locked up for some bullshit and she knows you're upset about it. Sometimes I can't stand her fucking ass."

"Mom, can we just try to have fun?" my cousin Sabrina asked. I think she could tell that I was upset enough without her mother making me feel worse.

"Don't tell me what to do girl! I'm the parent."

That's how it was in my family. Children were seen and not heard, and we were often brushed off. And the adults always made shit about themselves. It was my birthday, my dad was in jail, my mom was who knows where, and my day was ruined. I started to wonder how my young life had turned so bad so fast. Living without my dad for two weeks was like living in hell.

We continued on with my so-called birthday party, but there was nothing happy about it. My aunt tried to cheer me up by allowing me to open my presents, but it didn't work.

I got clothes, and my aunt gave me a pair of earrings. But the best presents would have been to have my mom & dad there. The two people I loved and adored were not around for my 10th birthday.

My aunt was really pissed.

"Your mother is such a bitch for leaving you high and dry on your birthday. She's probably somewhere sucking some dick. I hate that selfish bitch."

That did not make me feel better. My mom was not a selfish bitch to me.

Then to make matters worse, the gift from my dad was a cheesy radio. I knew my dad would never have bought it for me. My mom probably picked it out and put his name on it. I may have been young but I was smart and savvy enough to know that my dad would never buy me such a thing.

"Don't you wanna cut your cake, honey?" my aunt asked. "It's your favorite".

I always loved strawberry shortcake. But that day, I didn't feel like eating any.

After the cake was cut and all the gifts were opened, I called my mom, hoping that she was on her way to get me. I called again and again but she didn't answer the phone. I fell asleep on my aunt's couch.

I woke up to an argument. Aunt Toni and my mom were going at it.

"Katrina, why were you out with that fucking man when your man is in jail?" my aunt asked.

"Keep your voice down, bitch. Can't you see my child is sleeping?" my mom said. "I gotta do what the fuck I gotta do."

Do what she has to do. I had no clue what they were arguing about but my virgin ears continued to take heed.

"You know, Cappy said he may be able to help Marley get out of jail if I help him out a little."

"What you mean 'help him out'?" my aunt asked.

Silence filled the room.

"I know you ain't fucking with that herb-ass pig," my aunt said. "That pussy ain't gonna help get Marley out and you know it."

"I ain't fuck him. I just spent some time with him and kicked some bullshit on him so he'll help me out," my mom said.

"Yeah, right. I know you better then that, girl. You better watch your back."

I began to cry. Even though I did not fully understand, I knew something was happening with that cop and my mom.

When my mom came to get me, I pretended to be fast asleep. I had buried my face in the cushions to wipe my tears so she wouldn't know I had been crying. She woke me up and led me to the car. She and my aunt did not exchange goodbyes. In fact, after that night, I don't remember them speaking much on the phone or in person.

We arrived home to a sight that I would never have believed if it wasn't happening right in front of me. Cappy was standing in front of our house, not wearing his uniform, not sitting in a cop car.

I mumbled, "What the fuck is he doing here?"

My mom balled her fist and punched my underdeveloped chest with all her might.

"Keep your grown-ass mouth closed! This man is going to help daddy get out of jail."

"You do what he says, 'Mika, whatever he says. Do you hear me?"

I did not answer because she had knocked the wind out of me with the punch. When I looked up there was midnight looking in my window, reaching to open the door.

"Come on, sweetie. Let's go inside. Your mom says you've had a long day."

Who the fuck was he to call me sweetie and why was my mom telling this asshole who got my daddy locked up anything about me? And why was he at our house?

I paused but my mom nudged me so I had to get out of the car with his assistance.

"Tamika, Cappy is here because he felt so bad about what happened to your dad that he is trying to help us," my mom said.

"Help? We don't need his help," I blurted out as we entered the house.

"You need to control your child. Or should I put her in handcuffs?" Cappy said in a mean yet seductive way.

"I'll handle her, Cappy. You know how kids are these days."

She walked me to my room and told me to get my ass to bed fast or she would hit me again. I laid in bed wondering what had gotten into my mother and what my dad was thinking about at that moment. I prayed that he would come home soon and fix everything.

As I dreamt about my dad coming home, I felt a presence. I slowly opened my eyes. I got scared when I saw the whites of Cappy's eyes beaming down on me. Before I could scream, he covered my mouth.

"Listen, little girl. I'm in control now. You and your mom need me. I advise you to be nice to me or you will never see your dad again. His future is in my hands."

I could barely breathe. His beastly hands were smothering my nose & mouth. As my little body tried to maneuver out of his tight grip, I saw a shadow in the hallway.

Cappy quickly released me and turned all nice. "Good night, sweetie. Sleep tight."

I hated that word. Sweetie. I cried myself to sleep that night. I could not have imagined that Cappy would be the beginning of the end for me.

I prayed my daddy would come get me soon. I knew it was just a matter of time. So until then, I would obey my mom and say my prayers. Then the nightmare would be over.

I guess not all dreams come true.

My dad had been locked up for almost eight months. In the beginning, we visited him often, and my mom would tell me "Daddy will be home soon."

After a while, though, we stopped going to see him, and we saw Cappy more and more often.

I didn't tell my mom about Cappy's mysterious birthday message. I just sucked it up and tried to be as nice as possible. I wanted my daddy to come home. I needed my daddy to come home.

The long distance phone service had been cut off so my dad could not call me collect anymore. Mom and I were not doing good at all. We went from eating steak dinners to Oodles of Noodles. Sometimes three times a day. I remember my mom cried a lot about needing my dad and that God needed to get her out of this mess. She didn't talk to me much. I felt like she blamed me for daddy being away.

Cappy continued to come over. At first he would nap on the couch. But before long, he was staying the night. The next thing I knew, he was in bed with my mom.

One night I could not sleep, and it dawned on my young soul what was going on.

I had gotten up to use the bathroom, and as I walked past my mom's closed bedroom door, I heard her crying.

"Cappy, I can't do this anymore," I heard her say. "I love Marley. But he ain't never coming home, is he?" She was crying hysterically.

"Shut the fuck up, bitch! That nigga don't love you. He lied to you about everything. That's why he's still locked up. I can't help it that he is where he is. He better not drop the soap."

I hated Cappy. I wanted to go in there and kill him. My dad was my life. Why was my mom crying in front of that nigga like he was the truth? My dad was the man, in or out of jail. He did everything for us. Cappy didn't do shit for us.

I remember hearing Cappy laughing.

"You's a dumb bitch! Marley ain't comin' home no time soon. Now, after I fucked you and knocked you up, you gotta stay with me. You think Marley gon' take care of another man's baby even if he does come home?"

My mom started screaming then. "I hate you! I hate you! I ain't having this bastard baby! NEVER!!"

I thought to myself, BABY? I'm her BABY. What the hell was going on?

I huddled on the bathroom floor, which would become a common thing for me to do, and wondered what I should do next. I was only ten years old and had no clue about all that adult bullshit. All I wanted was for my daddy to come home and make my life perfect again.

I started to go back to my bedroom but I heard all this cussin' and screamin' so I opened my mom's door. Cappy had her on the floor, but I couldn't tell what was going on.

"You know you love this dick inside of you girl. Marley

can't fuck you like this. That's why I'm here and he's not."

"Please stop, Cappy! My daughter might wake up."

"She old enough to know what dick is!" he shouted.

I did not know then. But I learned in the next minute.

What Cappy was doing to my mom was the nastiest thing I had ever seen. I always had turned my head on the kissing parts in the movies. But it was my mom so I watched. It didn't look like she was enjoying what Cappy was doing to her.

"I'm gonna fuck you til you can't fuck no more."

"Cappy, I'm pregnant with your child! Have some respect!"

"I'll stop if you tell me you love me."

"Cappy, I love Marley," my mom cried.

A sigh of relief came over me. I could not understand why she was with Cappy in the first place. I wanted to go in the room and stop him but I was scared, so scared. I knew I would get into so much trouble. Maybe that's how grown people have fun, I reasoned. I had no clue.

After about ten minutes, I went back to the bathroom and flushed the toilet, hoping they would stop. I was wrong. It seemed like my mom's screams got louder and louder.

"Mom," I yelled. "MOM!" I yelled even louder.

"Yes, baby?"

"Are you OK?"

"Yes, baby. Go back to bed."

As I proceeded to my room, Cappy came out butt naked

with a hard dick and sweat dripping down his face.

"Excuse me, Tamika. I thought you were in bed. That's usually where little girls are at this time of night," he said with an ugly look on his face.

I ran to my room, locked the door and jumped under the covers. I was scared to death. All I could think about was my daddy and how he was so protective of me. I knew that if he knew what was going on, he would have killed Cappy.

Twenty minutes later, I heard a knock on the door.

"'Mika, baby, it's me. Open the door," my mom said in a low whisper.

I jumped up to open the door.

"Mom! Are you OK?" I hugged her tight.

"Yes, baby. I'm fine. We were just playing."

I knew she was lying. I could see the tracks of dried tears on her cheeks.

"Mom, when is daddy coming home?"

"Soon, baby. Very soon. I hope."

"Mommy, why is Cappy here? He got daddy locked up, and he's not treating us right."

"Baby, just a little while longer and we won't have to worry about him at all."

I had never seen my mom look so lost and alone. My dad was always there to help her. Now she seemed so helpless and desperate even to my young eyes. She kissed me on my head and told me to get some rest. I never even thought to ask if I was having a baby sister.

The next morning, I woke up to paramedics in my living room. My mom was on the couch and Cappy was holding her hand.

"Mommy, what's wrong?" I rushed to her.

"Everything is OK, 'Mika. Mommy just has to go to the hospital for a little while, OK?"

"Why?" I cried.

That's when Cappy came over to "rescue" me. But all I wanted him to do was die. I hated him and was embarrassed, especially because I saw his long black dick.

"Your mom is going to be OK, 'Mika. Just calm down."

My mom was taken by ambulance to the hospital. I stayed home by myself because Cappy said I was too young to know what was going on.

It was bullshit. I knew that whatever he had done to my mom had hurt her and hurt her bad. My mom hated hospitals. She didn't even go to see her favorite uncle when he was in the hospital dying from AIDS.

She must have really been sick. I cried until I couldn't cry anymore. I had no one to protect anymore and I had no one to protect me anymore. I started to believe that my daddy didn't care. If he loved me, then why didn't he break out of jail and come and save our family?

Later that night while I was asleep on the couch, I jumped when I heard the front door crack open. I cried, "Mommy!" but I soon realized it was not my mom. It was that black creature sent from hell.

"Shut up, girl. Your mom will be here in the morning. We'll go together to pick her up. Go back to sleep."

"Cappy, what's wrong with my mom?"

"She was having my baby and it died because your dad put a curse on it from jail. You see, Tamika, sweetie, me and your mom are together as man and woman. You know, boyfriend and girlfriend?"

I looked at him all confused. My mom and dad would never be apart. What was he talking about?

"Your dad doesn't want you anymore. That's why he hasn't called. He has no interest in you or your mom. So now I am going to be your dad. I'll take care of you, don't you worry."

"My daddy will be home soon. My mommy's only being nice to you so you can help him get out."

"Little girl, you have no clue about life. Your mom is a slut and you will be one too if a real man not a drug dealer like your dad doesn't step in and mold you to be what you are supposed to be. Go to bed, little girl."

"When my dad gets home, he's gonna fuck you up for being mean to me. I am his princess and my mom is his queen and you are just a piece of shit!"

As soon as the words left my mouth, I realized that I had gone too far.

Cappy came close to me and snarled in my ear, "GO TO BED, little girl, before I fuck you up."

I ran up the stairs and tried to lock my door but the lock was broken.

Oh no! What now? Think, Tamika. Think!

I ran and hid under my covers. I was crying and praying for my parents to come home.

After a while, I feel asleep. I felt a presence again but I did not move. I just laid still, hoping he would go away. He didn't.

I felt cool air on my legs as he lifted up the corner of my quilt. Then Cappy's big, black hand reached in my Sunday panties to touch my "pocketbook" as me and Mom called it.

My dad always told me not to let anybody go into my pocketbook, especially a man.

I really didn't understand what he was talking about at the time. But then all of a sudden I did.

Cappy's huge fingers slipped inside my pocketbook. He hurt me so bad but I was too scared to scream. I was mad at myself for not obeying my dad. And even if I had screamed, who would've heard me?

My mom was gone and my dad was in jail. It was just me and the beast.

As he touched what I would soon learn was my pussy, I heard him say, "Oh my God. This feels so good. I want this tight pussy."

I tried to peek out from under the covers to see what he was doing. All I could see was one hand in his pants and feel the other in mine. It was awful.

I knew he knew I was awake because I began to cry. But the louder I got, the more he seemed to enjoy it.

He pressed his fingers harder and harder inside of me until I heard and felt something rip.

I was burning. I pleaded with him, "Stop, Cappy! I want my daddy."

"Fuck your daddy! It's time for you to become a woman."

A woman? I was ten years old!

As I laid there being brutally molested by a grown-ass man, I began to say the Lord's prayer. "Our father, who art in heaven, hallowed be thy name…"

The next thing I heard was Cappy groaning loudly over my whisper.

"Oh shit! Oh shit! I'm comin'! I'm fuckin' comin'! AHH-HHHH! Damn!"

I didn't know where he was going but I was glad it was over. He pulled his hand out of me and left.

I laid there quietly crying to myself. I wondered how and why my life had become so messed up so fast. Had I been a bad little girl like my mother said I was sometimes? Did I deserve everything that was happening? Was I the cause of my family being in ruins?

As I laid there thinking, the beast came back in the room.

"Sweetie clean up," he ordered. "I think you're bleeding. You probably got your period."

I got up without a word and went into my dresser drawer and took out the pad from the packet we got in health class three months prior when we were taught about the birds and the bees.

I washed off, put the pad inside a fresh pair of panties, and got back into bed. I avoided the spreading blood stain on my sheets.

I knew then for certain that Cappy was truly the devil. I didn't understand before what a nasty motherfucker he was. He had fondled and molested my young pussy and didn't care about the blood or anything.

I was so ashamed. I didn't know what to do. I was too young to know what had happened to me. All I knew was that I was alone in the house with that black devil and it didn't feel good.

I felt the same way my mommy had looked the night before, bruised and hurt.

I started to wonder about what Cappy had said. Did my daddy not want me anymore? Maybe it was true. All I could do was think and cry and pray that if I was good, things would get better.

CHAPTER THREE

Still Falling

10 going on 11

That morning after Cappy molested me for the first time, he woke me up to pick up my mom from the hospital. Believe it or not, I was not happy about getting her. I thought she would know that I had done something wrong and call me a grown-ass. I was so scared he would tell her what had happened and that she would be mad at me.

Cappy and I rode in silence to the hospital. When we found her room, she was so happy to see me.

"Come here, 'Mika, baby. Did you and Cappy have fun without me?"

I thought to myself if that was fun then I don't ever want to have fun again. I know I had a look of shame on my face but I was too scared to open my mouth.

"What the hell is wrong with you, little girl?" my mom

asked in the way I hated.

"She became a woman last night. She's all grown up now," said Cappy arrogantly.

"What are you talking about?" Mom asked.

"Mom, I got my period," I said quickly before Cappy could tell her what had really happened.

She looked pissed but it wasn't about what I thought it was about.

"Your ass better not start with them damn boys neither!" she said.

I wanted to tell her, *Keep that man off me!* but I just sat there with my head down, wishing that Cappy had never come into my life. He took a part of me away when he arrested my daddy and then he took the rest of me.

I was a happy little girl before Cappy. But I found myself turning into someone no one knew, not even me.

Not once after we left the hospital did we discuss why she was there in the first place. My mom just chalked it up to female problems. She told me that I wasn't old enough to understand but one day I would. I had no idea what she was talking about but I didn't question her.

She was right about me not understanding. I didn't understand anything at all, especially not how she could so switch from being with a thorough-ass nigga like my dad to a punk-ass nigga like Cappy.

Time kept moving on. Almost a year had passed and it seemed like Cappy was there to stay. The phone calls from my dad became distant memories. I couldn't even remember the last time we went to see him.

I had lost it all in a matter of one year. My eleventh birthday was coming up but once again, all excitement was gone.

Cappy was staying with us on a regular basis. Thankfully, he had not touched me since my mom had been in the hospital, but he was always looked at me in the way an adult man should not look at a child.

Mom was oblivious to it all. All she seemed concerned with was throwing me a party with all my school friends.

"'Mika, Cappy's going to handle everything, baby," she said. "Don't you see that he's been taking care of us like your daddy used too? He's a good man. A good provider."

I remembered my daddy as loving and caring. Cappy had none of those qualities. He was a piece of shit. He wasn't getting daddy out so I didn't understand why was he still around.

I never used to have a problem speaking up because my daddy always told me to say what was on my mind. But I had become a different child, even in school.

I was positive that all my problems stemmed from my home life. Me and my mom had stopped kicking it because I hated talking to her after a while. All she ever did was praise the motherfucker who molested me and tried to fill my dad's shoes, something his punk-ass could never do.

Still, Mom was always catering to him and acting like he was the king of New York. Yes, he bought her stuff all the time and eventually started getting stuff for the house to make it like it was before daddy left. But none of it impressed me.

Cappy would say to me, "See, sweetie, these are the things you get when you work hard like a real man—like me."

I guess real men like to rape women and stick their man-size hand in little girls' pussies, too.

When he would say shit like that, I would go to the bathroom and throw up.

I did that a lot. I was just about eleven and probably weighed only fifty-five pounds. I was skinny but no one noticed or cared except the dumb little boys in class. They were always picking on me, saying I was on crack and shit. I hated them.

The day of my birthday, my mom took it upon herself to decorate the house and invite people from my school over. She knew I loved surprises. But then I had lost my taste for surprises. She tried to surprise me anyway.

"'Mika, it's your birthday! Look how me and Cappy decorated the house," she said excitedly. "Cappy bought all this stuff. You better be nice to him. Do you hear me?"

"Yeah, Mom, I hear you," I said dryly. "But could we talk

to daddy or go see him?"

"Listen little girl, your daddy left us with nothing. Mommy found somebody who is helping us and providing for us. You wanna go back to eating hot dogs & beans?

I remained silent.

"I didn't think so. You need to understand a women can't do it without a man. I tried, baby, but it just didn't work. The man is the provider. Can't you just try to get along with Cappy? I know you think he got daddy locked up but there's more to the story. And I'll be damned if I lose a good man over your bullshit, 'Mika. I don't have to explain shit to you anyway. That's your fuckin' problem, like it's always been, but your dad ain't never let me say shit to your spoiled ass. You're so ungrateful! I do all this shit for you and you give me your ass to kiss. Well, fuck you then, you little bitch."

I was used to my mom calling me out by name, but this was different. She was talking to me like I was a girl off the street, not like the eleven-year-old who loved her.

Well, I lost the little bit of love I had left for my mom that day. She had crushed the remaining ounce of spirit I had left inside my lifeless soul.

All my guests arrived but I didn't dress up or even get a little cute for them. I was not concerned with what they thought.

And all they could say anyway was, "You got a nice house. Dang, look at how big that TV is. I wanna play Pac-Man on that."

And there was Cappy, his yellow teeth smiling in the background like he was God or some shit. It should have been his birthday.

I wasn't beat for a lot of things that day. All I thought about was my dad. Every time the phone rang, I ran to get it but it was never who I needed it to be.

I needed love and the only person who was going to give it to me was my daddy.

I wondered if he was still alive. Was there something they were not telling me?

I felt abandoned by my mother and trapped by a man who had promised to bring my daddy back.

The party ended and so did any hope of hearing from my dad. I felt so lost. I really believed he would call me.

After the party, I went straight to bed. And once again, I heard Cappy and my mom going at it.

"Bitch, I did all this shit for your little bitch and she ain't even say thanks!"

"Cappy, she's a child. Leave her be. She just wanted a birthday call from her dad. She ain't mean no harm."

"What about how I feel? She humiliated me in front of all those kids. She didn't even acknowledge me."

He sounded like an ass. What type of man gets humiliated around a bunch of eleven- and twelve-year-olds? Only Cappy.

He was the type of man that needed to be recognized. My daddy was the type of man that was recognized. When my dad walked into a room, all heads turned. Cappy was noticed because he made himself noticed.

The days came and went so fast. Before I knew it, Cappy was nice and comfortable with my mom. He hit her and abused her and did whatever the fuck he wanted to. Women even called our house looking for him.

I always wondered why my mom was so stupid. I mean, my dad didn't ever do shit like that. She wouldn't have allowed it if he tried.

What was that man holding over my mom's head? Why didn't she put his ass out?

I didn't get it, and after a while I stopped trying. I stopped crying and stopped praying that things would get better. I became numb to everything. My dad hadn't called me and I hadn't seen him in two years. My old life was finished.

When I became a teenager, shit changed. I began to look out for myself because there was no one else and no one was going to change the way I felt. I began to distance myself from everyone.

Imagine life as a child with no friends or even family to turn to. I had no one, I had nothing and since I didn't have anyone to care for me or to care about, I chose the road to self destruction.

CHAPTER FOUR

No More Daddy's Little Girl

Age 13

"Girl get your ass down here & get ready to go to school!"

"I'm coming, Mom!" Then I whispered. "Damn! She gets on my fucking nerves."

I hated where I lived and I hated school. Shit, I hated life.

I ran downstairs only to see Cappy half naked on top of my mom right on the kitchen table.

I sighed loudly

"Umm, mmm. I think a child is in the room."

"You ain't no baby. You almost 14 years old. You're probably doing more than me and your mom," Cappy said snidely.

I ignored him and quietly ate a bowl of cereal. Then I got ready to catch the train to go to school.

"Hey, girl. You need some money?" Cappy asked aggressively as I was walking out the door.

"No," I whispered.

I always talked really low when I spoke to him. I had no respect for him but I was still a child and a little scared of him. Nah, I was a lot scared of him.

He screamed, "You better take this money. Don't be bitin' the hand that feeds you."

"If she don't want it, I'll take it," my mom said and winked at me.

Sometimes she would find a way to make me smile or just show that she still had a heart. I ran and grabbed the money.

"Hey, no thanks for your daddy," he said.

"Thanks," I mumbled. *Does he really believe he could ever replace my daddy?*

I didn't ask much about my dad anymore. Every time I tried, my mom would start crying and the next thing I knew, Cappy would start a argument with her.

I couldn't handle that. I loved her so much. She was my mother, good or bad. And overall she wasn't so bad. She was just doing the best she could.

I started to get more and more mad at my dad, wondering why he never called and why he never wrote.

Did he even care about me?

At that point it didn't really matter. Cappy was all we had, so I tried to make the best of it.

I went off to school as I usually did, hopping on the train. That day ended up like no other day.

I always met strange people in New York City, especially on my way to Manhattan.

That day on the train, an older white man stared at me the entire ride. I mean really hard.

At first I brushed it off like I normally did when people did that. I was a little funny looking but I had gotten a whole lotta form to my body over these last couple of years.

He kept gazing into my eyes like he loved me. I laughed because he made me blush.

"So, you are alive," he said.

"Excuse me?"

"I see you all the time and you look like you're always in a whole other world," he said.

"Not really. I'm not supposed to talk to strange white men on the train is all."

"What strange white man?" he asked. Then he looked down at his hands. "Oh my God! I'm white!"

"HA HA HA," I said sarcastically.

"Where are you headed?"

"School."

"Where you live?"

"I thought I told you I can't talk to you."

He came over and sat directly next to me in the crammed space between me and the lady that looked like Attila the Hun. Although I knew something was up with this guy, I was interested in him.

"What's your name, sweetheart?"

"Tamika."

"Well, Tamika, I'm John, and I am a strange white man. How do you do?"

"I do fine." I could not stop smiling.

"You have a wonderful smile,"

"Thanks."

"You are a beautiful girl. What high school do you go to?"

I thought to myself, *High school? Shit, I'm only in the 9th grade. Did I look like I was in high school?*

I played it off smooth though. "I can't tell you that, sir."

"No problem but let me at least guess your age. You must be 17, almost eighteen."

Even though I knew he was taking me for a loop, I still responded. "Yep, you guessed it."

"Are you a junior or a senior?"

"What? You writing a book or something?" I asked sort of as a joke but played along. "I'm a junior. My birthday comes late."

"I'm not trying to be nosy, Tamika. It's just that I'm a writer, producer and director, and I also do photography. I was just admiring your beauty and thought you were a model, but I see you're not. I'm sorry."

"I'm not trying to be rude, mister, um, John. It's just that strange people try and mess with young people, you know."

"I totally understand. I have young children of my own. But I'm actually on my way to my studio right now. Would you be interested in coming?"

"I can't go anywhere with you. Besides, I gotta go to school."

"Well, I'll do this then. Take my business card. Then talk to your mom and dad about me. Tell them I'm interested in working with you. You are a very pretty girl with a beautiful smile and a very nice shape."

He looked me up and down as if he were already in bed with me.

"I'll take your card but I'm not interested."

"OK, Tamika." he said as he got up to leave. "This is my stop."

He took my right hand, kissed it and told me how nice it was to meet me.

All day at school, I couldn't concentrate on anything All I could think about was how nice he was. No man had ever been as nice to me since my dad went away.

Damn. I wanted to go to his studio to just take a look. But I knew my mom, and she would not have any of it. After all, I was only thirteen. But he thought I was older. Damn! It was eating me up inside to think that an old white man was interested in making me a model.

Fuck it. I was going. Right after school. I would tell my mom that I had detention. That would buy me at least an extra two hours. She knew I had a smart mouth so I figured she would fall for the detention thing.

I called her from the pay phone at school, and as predicted, she fell for it.

"You make sure you bring your ass home as soon as it's over," she yelled. "It's crazy people out there. And don't be talking to no strange men."

She always said that but I never understood why.

When the bell ending school finally rang, I ran out the door and pulled out the fancy business card.

Shit. I was on my way.

John's place wasn't too far from my school so I found it easily. His studio was in a warehouse! I remember being a little scared when I saw the building.

I had lived a pretty sheltered life and hadn't experienced all that much. I was very naive. So I could not believe I was there.

I walked up a lot of steps then called out. "Hello! Is anyone here?"

"Yes, come on up."

I walked up a few more steps and then through a big

industrial-looking door. John was behind a fancy camera taking photos of a young girl. She wasn't my age, probably closer to eighteen or nineteen.

She was a white girl with a nice tan. I remember her wearing a lot of make-up. She was pretty, though, I guess. She just looked fake.

"Hey sweetheart! You came!" he said happily when he looked up and saw it was me. "I'm just finishing up with this shoot. I'll be right with you."

"OK," I said as I sat down on the leather couch.

I looked around and saw that the walls were covered with pictures of beautiful men and women. That cinched it for me. The guy was legit and I was going to be a star. I was already thinking about getting my dad out of jail and living happily ever after.

Thank you, Lord, I said to myself, thinking of how He made this blessing fall right into my lap.

When John was finally done with the girl, he began to focus on me.

"Let me fix you a cocktail so you can loosen up a bit," he said. "OK, baby?"

What the hell is a cocktail? I asked myself. *Was that what white people called their Kool-Aid?*

I said OK even though I didn't know what he meant.

I sipped the cocktail and liked it. It was fruity with a

slightly odd taste. But it was good.

"Now, Tamika, let me take your measurements. First you need to take your shirt off."

I was nervous but I did it anyway. I didn't want him to think I was a little girl or something.

He placed a tape measure around my hips, waist and breasts, making me feel a little nervous about what they were.

"So, are my measurements right?" I asked.

"Absolutely," he said while biting down on his lip.

"Can I have another drink please?" I asked.

I was feeling funny but I thought it must have been the sugar in the drink he gave me. I drank it too fast.

"So, Tamika. I think you would be good in movies since you've got all the right stuff," he said while handing me my drink. I tried to sip the second one slower.

"I can do movies?" I said, startled. "Damn, I never thought I was that pretty."

"Well, you are," he said. "Now I'll just take the camera out for fun."

"OK," I said since I didn't see any harm in it.

He began to film me. I gave him nothing but a smile. He kept saying "good job" but I wasn't doing shit. Then he came over to me and kissed me on the lips.

"Hey, John, I gotta go." I started to move backwards. "I

don't want my mom to worry."

"I'm sorry. I didn't mean to scare you off," he said. "I know you're still young yet."

I sat there thinking that I was letting him down. I had never kissed a man before and it didn't feel half bad.

"It's not that," I said, lying. "It's just that my mom worries a lot."

"I can give you money to take a cab if you want," he said.

"You would do that?" I asked.

"Of course, baby. I'm about to make you a star."

"Can I have another drink?" I asked.

"Hey, if you're looking to get toasted, I got something even better."

"What you mean by toasted?" I asked.

"I mean I don't want you to get sick from the alcohol. But the white shit won't do you like that."

I didn't know what the hell he was talking about again when he said "the white shit" but I finally got it that I was drinking alcohol. The alcohol my mom and dad drank was brown and smelled funny. That stuff he gave me tasted good and smelled good, too. But white shit? I was curious about what he meant.

"What's the white shit?" I asked.

"Cocaine, baby."

Then I knew exactly what he was talking about. We learned about it in school. I was nervous about chickening out if I didn't try it even though we were taught to stay away from it. But I wanted to be a star and rescue my dad.

I told myself that I had to do it. Shit, I'd seen white people on television doing it so I told myself that I'd do it just once, let him take my pictures and then leave.

He laid it out on the table and showed me what to do.

It was weird. I wanted to do it and never thought about the consequences.

As I tried the cocaine, I remembered my dad telling me to never fool with heroine. But he didn't say anything about cocaine.

I snorted it through my nose and a feeling came over me that was inexplicable. I felt dazed, like I couldn't move.

All I remember was John on top of me, taking my pants off. Since I felt paralyzed by the drug, all I could do was lay there, lifeless and clueless.

He was humping me up and down, up and down, but I had no feeling at all, not even pain. I felt kinda like a zombie.

After a while, when the cocaine wore off a little, I got up and got dressed.

John gave me $100 dollars and called me a cab. "Hey, baby. Come back so we can do the pictures, OK?"

"OK," I said. And that was that.

I got in the cab. And I was no longer scared of my mom or of Cappy. All I could think of was that I had just had sex and that I did drugs. It was unreal. It was like I was living outside of my life.

I got home and to my surprise, Cappy wasn't there. I ran to my room hoping my mom was already asleep. I was almost four hours late instead of two. I knew she was going to be pissed off at me.

She burst into my room. "Girl, where the hell you been? Cappy just went out looking for you."

"I told you I had detention."

"You should have been home sooner, girl."

"The train wasn't working, Mom, so I had to wait and then walk."

She came up close to me and started sniffing. I started feeling nervous.

"Oh my God, girl! You smell like sex and alcohol!" she exclaimed, amazed. "What in God's name where you doing, 'Mika?"

"Nothing, Mom." I started to cry and she hugged me.

"Baby go wash up. It's OK. I'll deal with Cappy. He's been looking for you. We're just gonna tell him someone attacked you, but you were too scared to say anything, OK?" She looked really worried. "Baby, you can't get pregnant, OK? You're too young. But I'll take you down to the clinic and get you some pills now that I know you're having sex."

What I couldn't figure out was how she knew everything! I didn't have a chance to say shit because all she cared about was how nervous and scared she was of Cappy.

I was thirteen and smelled of sex and alcohol. And all my mom did was say it was OK and was gonna get me some pills. Pills for what?

I grew up fast that day. Mom was as clueless as if she was the child instead of me.

And then I realized that she was careless. I mean whatever was going on with Cappy, my mom wasn't the mom I used to know. Cappy had her wrapped around his finger.

I showered and got back in the bed. She brought me some tea.

My high had settled down a bit, but I was still in a daze. I still felt so dirty even after the shower. I felt that I was not worth being around. All I wanted to do was go to bed and be alone.

Mom kissed me on the head and reminded me not to talk to Cappy. "Just act scared," she kept saying.

All I could do was try to fall asleep. But Cappy came home in before I was able to.

"I couldn't find her," I heard him say from downstairs.

"She's here, baby. Calm down, OK?" she said, trying to soothe him. "Somebody attacked her, Cappy," she said not even knowing if it was true or not because I never told her a thing.

"What? Someone attacked my little girl?"

"Baby, lower your voice. She's sleeping. She was all messed up. I just want her to get some sleep and wake up feeling better."

"I'll kill 'em," he snapped.

I remember thinking he was just mad because he didn't attack me first. Then I heard him crying.

He came into my room quietly, kneeled down beside my bed and whispered. I pretended to be asleep.

"Now, little girl, I know you ain't asleep," he said in a low voice. "And I know ain't nobody attacked you. You getting hot in the ass and you just needed somebody to fuck you. But remember, can't none of your little boys fuck you like a real man can, so watch your back."

Then he left the room. All I could do was cry.

Why was he on me like that? He acted like I was his child in front of my mom. And then he threatened me because all he wanted was to have me all to himself.

Everything in my life was weird. But I did know one thing. I never wanted to go back to John's place again.

I fell asleep feeling dirty, shameful, confused, like no one cared and that I was nothing. I couldn't wash off my feelings. And I certainly couldn't sleep them off either.

CHAPTER FIVE

Wrong Turns

Age 14

After that night, I was different. I was no longer just a little girl. I began dating boys. But not just dating 'em. I did 'em. I mean, I did 'em all.

I changed the way I dressed. I cut off the bottoms of my t-shirts and slashed the necklines to show more of my skin. I rolled down the waist on my pants so everyone could see my underwear. I stopped wearing my bra. And I stole some of my mom's make-up. I looked just like those chicks who hang around on the streets at night, which is to say I looked like a whore.

Cappy didn't stop me from dressing like that though. He even gave me money so I could buy some new clothes. And he was on my back trying to cop a feel whenever he could. Even his cop friends grabbed at me when Cappy's back was turned.

It bothered me but after a while I got used to it. And then I began to look for that attention in boys older than me. So I began dating, telling my mom I had detention pretty regularly.

I can't say I really liked the boys I had sex with. I was just so addicted to the attention that I could not help but have sex with them.

But none of them scared me like Cappy did, and I knew it wouldn't be long before he got to me again.

And when he does, I would tell myself, *I know he's gonna make it so I never forget it.*

One day after one of my escapades with a local boy, I came home and mom wasn't there. She was out shopping. But Cappy was there. He was on "vacation". But he didn't take us anywhere. He just sat his black ass on the couch and watched sports all day, drinking his smelly brown liquor. For real, I think he was playing the part of an undercover bum.

"Hi, Cappy", I said when I saw him. I started to run up the stairs before he could say anything but I was too slow.

"Hey, baby girl. That's all I get? What? No hug or kiss for your daddy?"

I walked over to him and kissed him on the cheek. My mom always reminded me not to upset Cappy. Then he grabbed me and stuck his tongue in my mouth.

"Damn, girl! You taste good," he said lecherously.

I pulled away from him, ran upstairs and locked my door.

Here we go, I thought. *He better not come in here. I wish my mom would hurry up.*

I started doing my homework. I was almost done with the eighth grade and high school was fast approaching. To my mind, high school was the big leagues so I was working on improving some of my habits.

I heard Cappy coming up the stairs and assumed he was coming for me.

I was right.

He knocked on my door. "Open up. I need to talk to you."

I didn't say anything, and I didn't open the door.

"If you don't open this door, I will kick the shit down!" he yelled. "Who the hell you think you is anyway locking some fucking door in my house?"

I remained quiet, praying silently to myself that he would just go away. Yet before I knew it, he did exactly what he said he was gonna do.

He kicked the fucking door open.

The nigga was insane.

He grabbed me off the bed and pressed me against the wall.

"You ready, baby?"

"No, Cappy. Please," I whined. "I don't want you to do

this."

"Don't start that 'please Cappy' bullshit with me! You fuckin' now so I know you're ready for a real man."

I had just sexed the boy from around the corner but I didn't say a word about it.

Cappy stuck his hand in my pants and began playing with me. As much as I tried to fight it, I couldn't because it felt good even though I didn't want it to.

Next, he did something to me that nobody had ever done. He laid me on the bed, pulled my pants down and put his face in my place.

He licked and licked and did all kinds of stuff down there. Then something weird happened to my body. I couldn't control it. It was like a crazy reaction came over me.

"You like it, don't you, girl? I knew you would."

I felt so ashamed because I did like it but I could not help it. It was all so weird.

He stood up. I thought he was gonna leave but he didn't. He was unzipping his pants.

He hovered over me and started pushing and pushing his big black dick against my pussy until he finally got it in. It hurt so bad, like he was ripping me apart. I tried not to cry but I was tearing up. All I could do was hope he would finish fast.

Suddenly, I heard movement downstairs. My mom had come home. *She'll make him stop,* I thought.

"Did you here that, Cappy?" I asked. "My mom's home."

Cappy didn't stop. It was like he wanted her to see us.

I started crying and begged him to stop. She called out both our names.

I would not dare let her catch us.

Cappy humped and humped. Finally he came inside of me.

"That was amazing, baby girl. I fucked the shit out of you. Now go tell your little boyfriend to fuck you like that!"

It was all so sick.

Cappy got up and ran to the shower. I hurried up and shut the door.

"'Mika, what the hell y'all doing that y'all can't hear me calling?"

My mom busted in the door and began looking around. I looked all messed up and I knew that she knew what was up.

"Where's Cappy at?"

"I think he's in the shower."

"Oh? So, what are you doing?" She was looking at me real funny.

"Just my homework, Mom. What you buy?"

"Nothing. I just went grocery shopping. Finish up that homework so you can eat your dinner."

"OK."

She knew something was up but she didn't say a word.

"Hey, babe. I ain't know you were home," Cappy said

when he got out of the shower. "What's for dinner?"

"Steak."

I could hear the anger in her voice.

Ooh, shit, she knows, I thought. *She's gonna kill me. I should have kicked him. I should have screamed. He's gonna tell her I wanted it. Oh boy, she's gonna put me out. What am I going to do?*

Mom and I were quiet during dinner. But not Cappy. He was so loud and animated like he needed to be heard.

"This steak is bangin', baby! Just bangin'."

The steak wasn't all that good. My mom overcooked it. But he was just kissin' up to her because he knew that she knew he had just banged her daughter. Yeah, he fucked her fourteen-year-old child.

Maybe I was just paranoid, though. Maybe that was it. Because if she knew, she would have been put his ass out.

I started thinking, *OK, now what?* I was unsure of what was going to happen next.

Nothing right away, at least. I ended up going upstairs and falling asleep. I had had a long day and my pussy hurt from fucking Cappy.

As usual, I woke up to them arguing a couple of hours later.

"Cappy, what did you do today?" I heard my mom ask innocently.

"I ain't do shit but chill, babe," he lied. "Why you so mad? Was you doin' something?"

"Cappy, did you mess with my daughter?"

I listened real hard to hear what he was gonna say.

"I should smack the shit out of you for saying some bullshit like that to me! What the hell is wrong wit you? She's like a daughter to me."

"Daughter, my ass, Cappy! I swear, I'll kill you if you fucked with my daughter!"

I was getting happy, thinking she was about to put his ass out. Then she started crying and mumbling something about my dad.

"Don't you ever bring that nigga up again, bitch! I'm about to kick your ass. I love you and Tamika, babe. I would never do anything to hurt either one of you. Now shut the fuck up wit that bullshit. If you think I did her, then go ask her.

"Maybe I will," my mom challenged him.

Next I heard boom, boom, bam and they were fighting. *Here we go again, I thought.*

I started to get up, but I asked myself why. She wasn't leaving his ass or kicking him out. So what would I be able to do? Nothing but cry, as usual. I was really good at crying. It became my thing. So I cried myself to sleep.

Later that night, someone came into my room. I prayed it

wasn't Cappy.

Out of nowhere, I felt a warm kiss on my cheek. When I turned around, I saw my mom.

Yes, I thought to myself.

"'Mika, baby. I love you no matter what, OK? I love you. Always remember that." She started to cry.

"What's wrong, mommy?"

"My life sucks. I hate being here."

I looked closely at her. She had red marks on her face.

"Mom, you gotta leave him. Can't you see he's a jerk?" It just came out. I didn't even care if she was going to get mad.

"You don't like Cappy, do you baby?"

"No, Mom, I hate him."

"Don't say that 'Mika. Don't you ever say that. You hear me?"

We were both quiet for a minute until my mom finally spoke. "Move over, 'Mika. I'm sleeping with you tonight." She laid down in my bed next to me.

I was so happy. Me and my mom had never been that close. But I always knew that she loved me—even if she did-n't always show me.

We slept that night with one eye open waiting for Cappy to come fuck with either one of us. And I think that night we could have taken him if he did. But he didn't make a move and that made the night even better. We didn't have a clue about what the morning would bring. And we didn't care.

The next morning when I had woke up, I heard Cappy's voice. But he wasn't yelling like usual. He was just talking in a normal way.

"Baby, I love you and I'm sorry for last night. You're the best thing that ever happened to me. But if you want me to leave, I will."

I was waiting for her to say "get the fuck out," but she didn't say shit. She just ignored him.

I ran to the bathroom and jumped in the shower before they could and stayed in for a whole hour without any interruptions. There was no doubt in my young mind that my mom knew exactly what had happened between Cappy and me. The question was what was she going to do about it? It wasn't long before I realized that she wasn't going to do anything at all.

I went to school as usual and didn't talk to anyone. I was funny about talking to people after what had happened with John. I didn't know why exactly.

After school I had nothing to do but go home. I didn't feel like messing with little boys. All I wanted to do was go home and sleep—forever.

My mom met me at the door and whispered in my ear,

"'Mika, put some clothes in your book bag fast and don't say a word. Cappy is asleep on the couch. Hurry up getting your things together and meet me outside."

I darted up the steps, grabbed a couple of things, and tip-toed back down. I managed not to wake Cappy up.

My mom was waiting for me in a red rental car. Strange. I jumped in the front seat next to her and she drove away like she was running for her life.

"Where we going, Mommy?"

"'Mika, trust me. We're going someplace safe. I have to protect you. That Cappy is a piece of shit. We're going to a shelter in Jersey."

Shelter? Jersey? Those two words kept on playing over and over in my head. Why were we going to a shelter when we have a house? And why the hell were we going to Jersey?

I remembered taking the same route to New Jersey with my dad. I remember going through a tunnel and then being on the New Jersey turnpike. Wow, it seemed like centuries ago. The memory made me realize how much I missed my dad but I dared not bring it up. I could see that my mom was upset. She looked like she had been crying all day. I didn't want to open my big mouth.

We got off at exit 14 but I had no idea where we were. All I knew about Jersey was that it was cheaper to live in than Manhattan and that a lot of people commuted to work in the city. I learned that at school.

I saw a sign that said Orange or East Orange or something like that. We pulled up to a secluded building deep in the woods. I was scared as hell. An older white lady came out to greet us. She looked around as if she were expecting trouble and hurried us through the door.

When we were safely inside, the lady asked my mom, "Did he try to follow you?"

"No. He was dead asleep when we left," mom answered.

"Good. I'll show you to your room and then you can get the rest of your things out of the car," the lady had said, sounding relieved.

"These are all our things," my mom told her matter-of-factly. "We won't be here long. Trust me."

The lady looked at my mom like she'd heard that one before and then finished saying what she needed to say.

"You'll share a room with Sheila and her daughter, Tina. Tina is five and Sheila is twenty and they are very nice. They will be here later on. Both are in school right now. You two will share this side of the room," she said, pointing. "Lunch is at noon and after lunch I will meet with you to go over the house rules here. In the meantime, make yourselves at home." She smiled kindly at us and left.

She never said her name or if she did, I missed it. But then I was in a daze.

The place was not bad but I had never shared a room with anyone before. To be honest, I was a spoiled brat and got whatever I wanted. Granted, we weren't rich. But we had a nice place to live in the city. Why did we have to leave? Why couldn't Cappy go back to where he came from? I was pissed.

"'Mika, don't put your stuff in that dresser. We ain't stayin' here long," my mom said as I started to settle in. "I just have to get my mind right for a minute."

"OK," I said despite not knowing what the hell my mom was talking about or what the hell she was doing. She was definitely buggin'.

We decided to check out lunch but it was some bullshit bologna and cheese sandwich that I would not eat. My mom told me to wait back at the room for our 3p.m. meeting.

I was so confused. I was hoping to pull my thoughts together but when I got to the room, I ran into a little girl and another girl who looked about my age.

"Hi," she said. "I'm Sheila and this is Tina."

"Hello. I'm Tamika and my mom, Trina, is probably somewhere smoking a cigarette," I said.

"Well, I can't wait to meet her," Sheila said. "I'll let her know how great this place is."

I rolled my eyes inside of my head but not so Sheila could see. I didn't want to be rude. I just thought she was talking nonsense. But that didn't stop her from talking.

"When my daughter, Tina, and I came here, we didn't know what to expect. But everyone here is like family. We stick together. So if you have an open mind, there's no limit to what this place can do for you."

"Is that right?" my mom said as she came into the room and extended her free hand to Sheila. In her other, she held a bag. "I'm Trina and I see you've already met my daughter, 'Mika."

"Yes, yes," Sheila said. "You have a lovely daughter. This is my daughter, Tina."

"Nice to meet you, Sheila and Tina," my mom said. "But we'll talk more later." She turned to me. "'Mika, let's go downstairs. I brought you some Chinese takeout."

Yes, I said to myself. *We can get away from these losers for at least a little while.*

As we ate in the lounge, I looked around and saw women and children in various stages of escape. Some looked rattled, unsure and shaken. Others looked strong and confident like they were ready to tackle the world.

I wondered if I'd ever feel that way. Since my dad got locked up, there wasn't much that I felt sure about, and I was too busy being weak to ever figure out how to be strong.

The worst part of everything, though, was I was always forgetting stuff. Sometimes I couldn't remember what had happened for days. I never told my mom, though. She would have told me that I was being stupid or lazy or something. I just kept it to myself and struggled hard to remember the things I'd forgotten.

After lunch, while we were wasting time sipping on our drinks, the older white lady found us.

"Hi Becky!" many of the woman sang in unison. That's how I learned her name.

"Hello, ladies," she said as she looked around the lounge.

"Hello, again," she said when she got to my mom and me. "I'd like to go over the house rules with you but right after this brief meeting, OK?"

"Ladies," she addressed the growing crowd in the lounge. "It's time for us to share. Remember, Dr. Barnaby is here to help you deal with your issues. Don't feel powerless about anything. You are all strong women and when you reclaim your lives, you will once again know your strength. Don't be afraid to let the magic happen. She's helped many of the women who've walked through the door before you and she can help you, too."

"Great," I mumbled under my breath to myself. "Now I know where Sheila got the BS from. I hope they don't think they're gonna brainwash me, too!"

For almost an hour, we listened as people poured their hearts out. And honestly, I heard some very touching stories. I felt like I wasn't the only person going through a bad time.

If they can make it, I thought, *I can make it, too.*

All was fine until Dr. Barnaby looked my way again. I noticed that she had been looking at me a lot during the meeting. Maybe she thought I was going to open my mouth. Anyway, she tried to involve me in the meeting by asking me a question.

"'Mika, you seem very moved by all this," she said kindly. "Is there anything you would like to share with us today?"

"She ain't got shit to say!" my mom broke in. I wasn't sure if she was talking to Dr. Barnaby or warning me.

"Oh, nonsense," Becky said. "The child is going through a rough time. You're her mother and I can tell that she loves you. Why don't you let her open up her heart?"

Becky's words calmed my mom. And since she was calm, I didn't feel there was a problem with saying a few words to get everyone off our backs. The problem, though, was that I didn't feel comfortable talking about personal stuff. Mom had always told me not to put our business out there on the street. So the only thing I felt safe enough to talk about were my memory lapses. I figured since Dr. Barnaby was a professional, I could maybe get some free help out of her.

"OK," I said. "I guess I can share." I looked at my mom for reassurance but it was like looking at a stone wall. I proceeded carefully.

"We've had some tough times but we've managed. The only thing that really frustrates me is when I forget things."

"Interesting," Dr. Barnaby said while rubbing her pen on her head. "What types of things do you forget?" She began jotting down a few notes on her pad.

"Types of things?" I asked to no one in particular. "I don't think I forget any types of things. I just forget. Period. I mean, I can go to school on Monday and then not remember anything else that week until Friday. And when I ask myself what happened to Tuesday through Thursday, I can't answer at all."

Dr. Barnaby looked very concerned and somewhat clinical. She whispered to Becky then jotted more stuff on her pad. Finally, she looked up at me.

"OK, 'Mika," she started calmly, "you may not believe this but I think I can help you with your memory lapses."

"For real?" I asked, perking up for the first time since we got to the place.

"Yes, for real," she said. "If you're game and if your mom doesn't have any problem with it, we can start right away."

"Please, mom," I said turning to her.

"Yes, please, Trina," some of the other women in the room joined in.

"I guess it's OK," my mom said. "Her fast ass is always coming up with something." Many people in the room gasped. "It'll be interesting to see what 'Mika's going to say

"It's alright, ladies," Becky interjected. "I haven't gone over the house rules with Trina yet. She doesn't know that cursing isn't allowed in the house. Let's forgive her this time."

My mom looked at Becky with a 'you've got to be kidding me' expression on her face but didn't say anything. I started wondering, though, if we'd make it through a day in the house. My mom was always cursing me out about something.

"OK 'Mika," Dr. Barnaby said, interrupting my thoughts. "Your mother said it's OK so let's get started. You'll need to sit right here next to me." She tapped the empty chair next to hers.

I sat in the chair cautiously despite being eager to find out the reasons behind my memory losses. There were too many things that I needed explanations for. And, hopefully, I was about to get them.

CHAPTER SIX

Marley's Deportation to Kingston, Jamaica

Age 14

Dr. Barnaby pushed play on her CD player and the lounge filled with soothing music. It was like we were in the woods with chirping birds, the wind blowing through the trees, and a babbling brook running nearby.

Next, she took a florescent watch from her bag and began to swing it from side to side from a short length of rope. She asked me to concentrate on its ticking not on its colors. Of course I concentrated on its changing fluorescent color. But before I knew what was happening, I started to feel different. I felt removed from the room we were in even though I could still hear Dr. Barnaby softly talking to me.

"'Mika, are you with me?" she asked.

"'Mika? 'Mika's just a scared little girl," said a voice that sounded similar to mine. "I'm Tammy. Tammy's runs the show. She's the one who makes sure Mika's soft little ass doesn't get harmed anymore."

"And how was she harmed before?" asked Dr. Barnaby.

"Please," Tammy said. "She's been harmed by everybody who supposedly loved or cared about her."

There were gasps around the room. Becky shushed everyone.

"And how did these people harm her?" Dr. Barnaby asked.

"Her dad deserted her," Tammy said. "Cappy and his partner violated her and all her mom ever said was to 'grow up.'"

"Wait a moment," Dr. Barnaby said. "Who is Cappy? And what type of business is he in to have a partner?"

"Cappy is the pig that locked up 'Mika's dad," Tammy said. "Then he had the audacity to show up at her front door trying to holla at 'Mika's mom. Any other bitch would'a spit in his face but not Trina. She took him in and started fucking the man who got her husband locked up. Then she didn't do shit but listen to everything he told her to do. She even kicked 'Mika out of the house sometimes for days."

"That's a lie," Mom shouted.

"It's the goddamned truth!" Tammy snapped. "And if it wasn't for her forcing 'Mika to be on the streets, Cappy's nasty-ass, fat fucking partner wouldn't have raped her."

"I didn't know about that," Mom shouted. "I would have

done something."

"You lying bitch!" Tammy shouted. "You knew! You just didn't want to know. You didn't care. You never had any time for 'Mika. Your head was so far up Cappy's ass that you couldn't tell whether or not 'Mika was coming or going. And you wouldn't have done shit anyway. You said the same shit when you found out that Cappy had raped her the first time."

My mom sobbed loudly.

"What did she say?" Dr. Barnaby asked.

"She cursed Cappy out until he threatened to leave her if she wouldn't let him fuck her daughter whenever he felt like it. So next thing you know, she comes into 'Mika's room and tells her that it's time for her to stop crying and be a woman. She told her own daughter that she had to do what she had to do to make sure they both survived."

"That's a lie!" Mom yelled.

"It's not a lie!" Tammy yelled back. "It's some sick shit but none of it is a lie."

"That's it. I'm sick of this shit," Mom yelled. "I don't know what kind of game you're playing here Dr. Barnaby but it stops now. Snap her out of this shit so we can get the fuck out of here. We're leaving right the fuck now!" Mom yelled.

But Dr. Barnaby didn't make a move. Instead, she did something and before I knew it, I was back in the room. Mom was standing in front of us with tears in her eyes and her fists balled up. Then uniformed guards approached us.

"What happened?" I asked but didn't get an answer.

"Trina," Becky said. "Where are you going? You know it would be irresponsible of us to let you leave here until we get to the bottom of this."

"Fuck what the hell you're talking about!" Mom yelled. "This is my motherfucking daughter and ain't a goddamned soul gonna take her away from me!"

"No one is trying to take your daughter from you, honey" Becky said. "We just want you to relax and stay with us a while."

"What's going on is we haven't even been here a day and you're fucking my daughter's head up," my mom said. "I don't think this place will do her or me any damned good. You won't drive me the fuck crazy."

"Ma'am, you are really gonna have to watch your language in front of the children," one of the officers said.

"I don't have to stay in front of these kids," my mom said. "I can get out of here with my own kid and let y'all keep screwing up people's minds."

"Trina, please, just relax," Becky said. "It will take us no time to get to the bottom of this and if you still want to leave, you're welcome to."

"You ain't got to be telling me what I can do," my mom snapped. "I'm a grown-ass woman. I'll leave whenever the hell I please."

"You're right, ma'am, you are an adult," the officer said.

"But the child is a minor," he added. "And she isn't going anywhere until we have guarantees that she'll be safe wherever she goes."

"Oh, I get it," my mom said sarcastically. "Y'all are trying to take my daughter away from me so y'all can brainwash her. Well, y'all just fucked with the wrong bitch, the wrong bitch! You hear me?"

She pushed the officer out of her way and started stomping towards the door.

"Mom! Where are you going?" I yelled with tears welling up in my eyes.

"Don't worry, 'Mika. I'll be back," Mom said. "Just be strong. I'm gonna make sure they don't screw your head up any further."

"No, Mom. Wait!" I yelled and ran after her. But I was stopped. One of the officers grabbed me and wouldn't let me leave.

"Believe me, it's for your own good," Dr. Barnaby said.

"No! I want my mom. Mom, please don't leave. Let me go! Mom wait for me! Please. Wait for me."

It didn't matter how much I cried, pushed, pulled or continued with my temper tantrum. No one heard me. My mom was gone. She'd left me somewhere in the boondocks of New Jersey.

When I later realized my predicament, I ignored what people

were saying to me and went back up to the room to lay down. I wanted to sleep forever. I'm not sure if it was for forever but eventually I did fall asleep and dreamed I was back at home with my mom and dad and we were a family again.

But I wasn't in New York City when I woke up from the dream.

I dragged my beaten body and soul out of bed and looked at Sheila and Tina like I wasn't beat. They tried to strike up a conversation but I just smiled at them.

I left the room and started wandering around the complex.

I stopped outside a TV room and looked inside. A few women were watching the news.

Watching TV could have taken my mind off things but I needed to watch something funny. The five o'clock news normally didn't interest me. It was always just a bunch of bull about black on black crime and political bullshit that I couldn't care less about.

Yet a face splashed across the screen grabbed my attention. The man reminded me of my father. Then I realized it *was* my father.

I rushed into the room and plopped down on the couch and listened to the news report.

"Jamaican immigrant and naturalized citizen Marley Jefferson is being deported back to his native Kingston,

Jamaica, to stand trial in that country for what he has been convicted of in this country. The unprecedented decision by the Supreme Court to allow Jefferson's return to his home-land shocked many law makers. Yet in light of the seriousness of Mr. Jefferson's crimes, most feel the decision was just.

Jefferson has been convicted on a multitude of drug charges, murder, kidnapping, and illegally laundering over one hundred twenty-five million dollars. Over his twenty-five year drug trafficking career, it is estimated that Mr. Jefferson has smuggled close to six tons of illegal drugs into the United States.

His conviction is a huge victory for the D.E.A. in its war on drugs and will more than likely be a huge setback for the drug cartels operating all along the eastern seaboard. As for the fate of Mr. Jefferson, we will wait and see."

I was stunned. I stared at the television for a long time after, seeing nothing but my dad's face. I was truly living the day from hell. And I thought I'd already hit rock bottom.

After a while, I got off the couch and resumed roaming around the complex. I wasn't beat to speak to anyone. All I wanted to do was drown in my own misery. I couldn't understand what I—a fourteen-year-old—could have done to deserve half the things that were being thrown at me in my life. And I wondered if my bad luck was over or if it was going to keep following me around.

BOOK TWO

Recovery

CHAPTER SEVEN

Promises Broken

I spent two months at the center and my mom called me only twice. She didn't visit or send me money. It was like I no longer mattered to her.

My sessions with Dr. Barnaby helped me remember many of the things I'd forgotten. One of the things was the money my father sent every month since he was locked up. He'd told me numerous times that he was sending a thousand dollars a month.

Dr. Barnaby told me that I had repressed memories that were too painful or caused me more trauma than I could bear.

She also told me that I was suffering from a form of schizophrenia that is caused by post-traumatic stress. The girl, Tammy, that spoke out that first day was a psychological defense mechanism. My mind created Tammy to protect me when she thought I was too weak to protect myself.

So that explained why days would go by and I would

have no memory of what I'd done. Tammy had taken over. I guess some things are too painful to remember, just like Dr. Barnaby said.

Of all the things I'd been through, what baffled me most was why my mom bothered with Cappy at all. Our house was paid off and dad was sending her money. She didn't need Cappy hanging around, being a complete asshole and being mean to us.

It's no wonder why I had so many problems, especially in school. But, thankfully, I've been doing great in school at the complex.

I almost made the honor roll last marking period. I thanked Miss Becky for that. She made sure I went to school every day and even hired a tutor for me so I could get a head start on high school work.

Little by little, I got myself together. It was rough, though. I'd been through so much for my age. But I realized that my life didn't have to end in tragedy just because it started that way.

One day, at the end of my tutoring session, I heard a ruckus in the lounge. So being my nosy self, I peeked my head inside before going upstairs for a nap.

I was immediately taken aback. It was my mother pitching a bitch to Miss Becky.

"She's my fucking daughter and you can't stop me from

seeing her!" Mom snapped.

"No one is trying to keep you from your daughter, honey, but you have to understand that you've been gone for over two months. I had to get temporary custody just to be able to care for the child," Becky said as nicely as she could. "You would be so proud of her if you saw her progress. She almost made the honor roll last marking period." Miss Becky was cordial and logical but my mom wanted no part of it.

"Fuck your honor roll!" she yelled. "My daughter has been on the honor roll plenty of times."

"You're right about that," Miss Becky said. "We looked up her records and saw that she's been on the honor roll before—but not once since her father was put in jail."

"Are you trying to say I'm not a good parent?" Mom hissed with her nostrils flaring.

"No. What I'm saying is that Tamika has been in obvious pain since her father's been away. And we've been helping her deal with that pain." Miss Becky was still trying to be cordial.

"Well, right now you need to help her deal with the pain she's in from missing me. How 'bout that?" Mom snapped. "I want to see my daughter right now. I don't have time to keep playing stupid games with you."

"I don't see how your daughter's well-being is a stupid game, Trina," Miss Becky countered.

I finally decided to end their conversation before it escalated to something bigger.

"That's OK, Miss Becky," I said as I walked into the lounge.

"Oh, my baby!"

Mom ran to me and hugged me. I didn't hug her back. Her breath smelled of liquor and it was early in the afternoon. "Have they been treating you good, baby?"

"Yes. I haven't felt so good and so safe since daddy left," I said. I knew it was a blow but I didn't care.

"Yeah. Times have been hard for us with him not around."

"I never cared about that, Mom. All I ever cared about is you and me—working things out together, on our own," I said, trying to reason with her.

"And we will, baby," Mom said. "Our lawyer says that you'll be back with me a couple of weeks. We have to go to family court and then we'll be back together. I promise you I haven't forgotten about you. I've been pulling my hair out battling for you. It just takes longer for stuff like this than we think."

"Mom, I hope you've heard me," I said. "I only want to be with you if it's just me and you. I'm prepared to testify if I have to that Cappy raped me."

"Hush your mouth, child, with that nonsense," she warned. "You are just like your dad. Y'all always think you know everything but sometimes you don't know what's going on. Sometimes you have to stop trying to fight and start trying to survive. Talk like that is not safe, baby. You need to be more careful about the things that come out your mouth."

I took that as a warning from Cappy even though it came from my mom's mouth.

"Mom, I'm not scared of Cappy," I said. "After all I've been through, I'm not scared of anybody. And you're right, I don't know everything. I may not have any control over whether or not the court will allow me to stay here. But I do know that Cappy raped me and you let it happen. Now everyone here, Miss Becky and all the other women watching and listening right now, knows that I don't want to go back with you unless it's just me and you. No Cappy, Momma. I can't and won't be around him. I refuse to. But if I am ordered to go back home and he's still in our house, I promise you, the next time he touches me will be his last time. By the way, where is he?"

"He's out in the car, baby," she said. "Do you want to go say hi to him?"

"Hell no! Haven't you heard a word I've said?" I shouted with my nostrils flaring. "And what's wrong with you, Mom?" I was shocked. "Abusers aren't supposed to know about our secret location! You broke the code, mom. You've put every woman and child here in jeopardy."

"Child, no one is in jeopardy," Mom said. "He's harmless. And he's a good man. I feel safe with Cappy. He's gonna marry me so I can get my green card and then we'll be a family."

"Mom, I guarantee you that you are the only mother here who would call the man that raped her daughter a good man and consider him to be harmless. And you're talking about marrying him. Please!" I was livid.

"Let me tell you one thing," Mom said, getting angry herself. "I am still your mother and you will not sass me. I brought you in this world and I can take you out of it. Do you understand me?" she yelled. "Do you?"

"Yes ma'am," I answered, remembering to show respect as I was taught in the sharing sessions. She was still my mother and I did have to treat her as such—even if she was acting like a stupid child.

"Good," she said, calming down a bit. "Then we understand each other. Give your mom a hug before I leave. Like I said, soon we'll be back together."

I hugged her and tried to fight back the tears that were forming in my eyes. I couldn't even think about living in the same house as Cappy again. I wasn't sure if mom had been brainwashed or if she was just brain dead. But I was sure that she was about to strip away all the progress I'd made.

CHAPTER EIGHT

Welcome Home Marley

As she promised, Mom showed up again two weeks later to tell me know about our court date. But I already knew. Miss Becky had told me, and Dr. Barnaby had already counseled me on how not to fall apart if things did not go in my favor.

"Don't ruin your life over some asshole," Dr. Barnaby had said. I laughed because I never heard her curse before.

I took a deep breath and peeled myself out of bed. There was no use in prolonging the inevitable. I had to go downstairs and talk to my mom even though it was hard for me to respect her at that point. For the life of me, I just couldn't understand how she allowed herself to stay with Cappy.

"My baby," Mom said when I walked in the meeting room.

"Hi Mom," I said, giving her a weak hug.

"You look so good, so grown," she said.

"I've been eating well lately," I said, delivering another stab without appearing to get smart.

"I can tell," she said, laughing. "Well, I came here to let you know that we'll be going to court in a couple days. Soon you'll be back with your mom where you belong."

"That would be great mom," I said, knowing I was about to flip the script. "I got Miss Becky and Dr. Barnaby to get the right judge so they can get a restraining order against Cappy as a condition of my returning to the house…"

"You did what?" she asked, angrily.

"Yeah, Mom. He won't be able to bother us anymore," I said matter-of-factly. "It will be just you and me—the way it was always supposed to be."

"'Mika, did I not tell you that Cappy and me are getting married?" she asked. "He's gonna help me get legalized. I'm gonna be a citizen."

I sat silently staring at the wall so she changed the subject.

"So, baby, I hear you're getting all ready to go to high school in the fall?"

"Yes, ma'am," I said. "It's going be great. Everything is exciting to me. I've been learning so much."

"You were always smart, baby," she said. "Well, I gotta go. Cappy's waiting for me. You know I love you, girl." She hugged me. "You stay strong. Justice is coming soon and we'll be back together."

I watched her walk out the door, back to Cappy. Miss Becky approached me as soon as she was gone.

"You did good, 'Mika," she said. "But I really wish you didn't mention anything about what we're trying to do. I know you were probably just calling her bluff, but I'm not sure how she'll handle the news. Sometimes it's best to keep people in the dark about things."

"I'm not sure if my mother could find her way out of a wet paper bag right now," I said. "Did you smell her? She was drunk again. She used to always argue with Dad if he came home drunk but now she's the lush. I hope she doesn't turn into a bum just like Cappy."

"Well, all you need to know is that everything will work out exactly the way God wants it to," Miss Becky rationalized. "If you look at things that way then you'll be able to continue getting stronger regardless of the obstacles." She hugged me and ruffled my hair with her hands. "Oh, I almost forgot. I saw your father on the early news this morning."

"Did you really?" I asked excitedly.

"Yes, I did," she said. "And since I knew how much you'd want to see it, I taped it for you. You can go watch it on the DVD burner in the media room."

"Oh, thanks, Miss Becky," I said, hugging her again. "That's just what I need—a dose of Dad to counteract all the crap I'm feeling about Mom and Cappy."

"Crap, 'Mika?" Miss Becky said.

"I'm sorry, Miss Becky," I said with a smile as I ran towards the media room.

The news story was about my dad but mostly it was about how diplomatic relations between the US and Jamaica might be damaged if my dad wasn't punished for his crimes here in the US.

But I saw my dad's beautiful smile and handsome face as he shook hands with various Jamaican politicians and dignitaries. Apparently, he was being thanked for the donations of money he had given to the Jamaican people over the years.

The scene seemed to me like a Welcome Back to Jamaica Party. It didn't seem like punishment. I guess that's why the US government was so pissed.

But, they'll get over it, I thought. *He's my dad.*

I also learned from the news story that my dad owns three office buildings and nineteen homes in Jamaica. And has over seven and a half million British pounds—approximately six million US dollars—in The Bank of London.

"Damn!" I whispered to myself as I ejected the DVD.

Three days later, I was in family court with Miss Becky. The courtroom was cold and impersonal, a place people weren't supposed to leave from happy.

I was shocked to see black-ass Cappy sitting in the row

right behind my mom.

He has some fucking nerve, I thought.

Mom's lawyer looked like the devil's advocate, or at least what I that would look like. He was, after all, trying to get me back into the same house as Cappy and ruin my life.

The judge was an old white man. He looked like one of those angry opponents of the civil rights movement that I've seen on television every year around Martin Luther King's birthday.

Miss Becky, though, didn't seem moved. "We have an open and shut case," she said.

I just prayed that things would go as easily as she believed. It had been proven that nothing every went smoothly for me.

Court proceeded as expected with both sides presenting arguments for my staying with them. Then it was my turn. I started to feel nervous. Miss Becky tugged on me and told me that I was the next and last witness.

"If you want to be free from that devil, honey, you are going to have to help yourself win your case," she told me.

I took a deep breath and crossed my fingers.

When Miss Becky's attorney said "no further questions" after completing her re-direct of the person on the stand, I sighed. It was time for me to do my thing.

"Your honor, the defense calls Tamika Jefferson," the attorney said.

I got up and walked slowly to the stand.

"Do you swear to tell the truth, the whole truth, and noting but the truth?" the court officer asked me as he placed a Bible in front of me. I had seen other witnesses place their hand on the book but I couldn't do it.

"I'm sorry," I said, "but I can't swear on the Bible."

There was a slight chuckle from some people in the courtroom so the judge hit his gavel several times.

"Order in the court!" he said before turning to me. "That's quite alright. You do not have to swear on the Bible if you choose not to. But do you affirm that everything you say hear today will be the truth?"

"Yes, sir, I affirm," I said. "I promise to tell the truth about everything."

"Good," he said. "You may proceed, Counselor."

The officer walked away with the Bible and Miss Becky's attorney took the stage.

CHAPTER NINE

Letter from Kingston, Jamaica

"Tamika, can you tell me where you've been living the last few months?" Miss Becky's attorney asked.

"I've been at the Strength in Numbers Women and Children's Shelter in Orange, New Jersey." I said.

"And who has been caring for you since you've been there?"

"At first Mom was there with me," I said. "But she stayed only one afternoon. Since she left, Miss Becky has pretty much been doing my mom's job."

"Objection," my mom's attorney shouted.

"Sustained," the judge said regarding my low blow. "You are not able to give us your personal opinions. Just tell us the facts."

"OK," I said, happy that I had accomplished what I had intended to.

"So, Tamika," Miss Becky's lawyer continued, "is there a reason why your mom left?"

"Yes, sir," I said. "Dr. Barnaby hypnotized me to help me figure out why I was having memory losses. It turns out that I have a problem called schizophrenia. A person named Tammy takes over my body when I'm in danger and scared. Tammy took over that day in front of my mom and told how she let him rape me," I pointed to Cappy.

"Objection," Mom's lawyer yelled.

"Mom got mad because Tammy was telling the truth. So she left…"

"Objection, your honor," Mom's lawyer yelled again.

"Sweetheart," the judge said to me. "When the lawyer says objection you are supposed to stop talking until I rule on the objection. OK?"

"Yes, sir," I said. I was playing the sweet and innocent roll to a tee.

"Now," the judge said. "Your objection is sustained, Counselor. Tamika, you are not able to speak about what you think someone else is thinking about. Understand?" He looked my way then looked at Miss Becky's attorney, giving her the go ahead to continue.

"So, Tamika," she continued, "what happened after Tammy took over your body and accused your mom of letting Cappy rape you?"

"Well, my mom argued with Miss Becky. Miss Becky did

not want me to leave until we all got to the bottom of the things I had said under hypnosis. Miss Becky said she couldn't allow me to be put back in danger until she found out where my mom was going. She said she didn't want me to be around Cappy until he was investigated. Miss Becky said that anything else would be irresponsible of her and the shelter. If my mom wanted to leave, she had to leave by herself."

"So did your mom leave without you?"

"Yes. She left that day and promised to come back," I said.

"Well, did she come back?"

"Yes. She came back about two months later," I said.

Several people in the court ooh'd and aah'd so the judge hit his gavel again.

"I'm about to clear this court room if you can't control yourselves," he warned. The court quieted down,

"Wait just a minute, Tamika," Miss Becky's attorney said. "Did you say that your mom left you after learning that you were raped by her friend and didn't come back for over two months?"

"Yes. She didn't come back for over two months."

"Well, did she at least come back with the rapist in a body bag?"

"Objection!"

"Withdrawn."

"No, she didn't. He's right over there." I pointed at Cappy

again.

"Objection, your honor," Mom's lawyer said.

"Sustained," the judge said. "Tamika, did you forget what I told you before about objections?"

"I'm sorry, sir," I said, sounding shaken. "It's just hard for me to concentrate and remember with that man staring me in my face."

"Your honor!" Mom's lawyer hollered.

"The court will take a ten minute recess," the judge said then hit the gavel on the table.

When the judge came back into the courtroom, he addressed us quickly and precisely.

"This case will be postponed for two weeks while some of the charges are either disproved or substantiated. And when we resume in two weeks, the defendant is instructed not to bring along anyone other than a family member. This is family court."

He hit his gavel once more on the table and that was that. I was safe for a little while.

When I was safely back in my room at the shelter, I was bubbling with joy. And then Miss Becky's secretary came to my room and handed me a letter postmarked from Jamaica. My dad had finally written to me! I was so excited.

Dear Tamika:

Time has been so unkind to me for not allowing me to see or hear from my baby for so many years — especially since I was arrested on trumped-up charges in the first place. But that's the game you have to play when you choose the profession I chose. Still, some things just aren't right for Jakes to do regardless of what line of work someone is in. So now that you're old enough, it's time I filled you in on the truth about why I got arrested in the first place.

The slimeball who arrested me, Cappy, turned out to be the crooked cop one of my lieutenants was paying off. But when things got hot for Cappy with Internal Affairs and the Drug Enforcement Agency, he set my lieutenant up, busted him and stole over two hundred thousand dollars from him in the process. And that's where he fucked up. The Jakes I paid out were much higher up in rank than Cappy and so he knew that eventually I would let them know that something was wrong with his math the day. Cappy turned in some of the drugs and cash that he confiscated in the bust but not all of it. So he killed someone with his back-up gun and planted it in the car after he stopped us that day. I was set up.

And about the supposed stolen car—this is the most painful part to tell you. INS had been giving me the runaround for years when I tried to get a green card for your mother. Still, they couldn't stall forever and I told your mother as much. I guess she didn't listen to me. She chose to listen to Cappy. He threatened to have her deported if she didn't help him and promised to assist her to get her green card if she did. So she called the Jakes and reported my car stolen to give Cappy a reason to stop me. Yes, you read me right. Your mother was involved in my getting locked up right from the beginning. Cappy got to her. And for whatever reason, she didn't have enough faith in me to believe that I would get her her green card. She trusted that damned Cappy instead and brought a lot of unnecessary pain and struggle into our family — not to mention that she also put at risk my business, the drug cartel that I run, that's earned nearly a billion dollars over the years.

But all isn't lost. I've been in contact with my Jakes in the police department and at the DEA the entire time I was locked up. I helped them build a solid corruption case against Cappy. They even devised the scheme to have me deported so that Cappy wouldn't suspect anything. Yes, he's shaken now after the televised welcome I got upon my return to Jamaica. The Jakes will move in on him based on my information. But he's probably more concerned about me getting on his ass for the fucked up shit he's done to our family and for my connections gettin' pissed about all the money the cartel is losing out on because of him covering his ass.

Whatever the case, Cappy will be dealt with by the law. That has to be his biggest fear. He's fabricated so much evidence over the years that the inmates he's gotten locked up will be dying to see his ass for something the second he walks through the prison gates.

Now, enough about Cappy. How is my little girl? I'm sure you're not so little any more. I regret missing just one day of your life and I've missed too many. Soon, though, we will be in touch and I will be able to stroke your beautiful face. Until then, stay strong, and know that you're dad loves you and is always here for you. And I can't wait until I'm able to make arrangements to see you. It won't be as long as you think.

Your dad,
Marley

Tears were flowing from my eyes when I finished reading the letter. But they weren't like the tears I cried at the house after dad left and Cappy showed up. They were happy tears. Knowing that my dad still loved me and hadn't forgotten about me meant the world to me.

I hated Cappy all over again with a level of disgust and loathing I'm not sure any mathematician could compute. I despised him. And I wasn't too happy about mom either. My perfect life fell apart and they were equally to blame.

But I was happy that the God I thought had forgotten about me was giving me a second chance at life. I was happy for the first time in so long. I felt I could finally breathe a sigh of relief and relax a little bit. My life was going to come together.

CHAPTER TEN

Vengeance Is Mine

Two weeks later

Just when I though things were coming together, everything fell apart.

We went back to court and the judge ordered me to be returned to my mom's custody under certain conditions. Cappy wasn't allowed to be anywhere around me. He issued a restraining order that was to be reviewed in six months. Until that time, Cappy wasn't allowed in the house that my dad had bought.

You would have thought that I'd have been happy, right? It's what I'd wanted all along. But I wasn't happy. Miss Becky told me all about restraining orders and how men ignored them. "There are so many stories, honey. Women with restraining orders against their ex-husbands or boyfriends still end up murdered. It's a crying shame. You'd just better be careful and don't hesitate to call me."

And I had every intention on calling Miss Becky if I had to. But I knew my mom and was sure she'd watch me like a hawk.

And when I got back home, that's exactly what she did.

I couldn't go anywhere without her. She walked me to school. And when I got out, she was waiting to pick me up. She had a private investigator be my bodyguard on a part-time basis. He was allowed to follow me around in school as long as he didn't bring his gun on the premises. Mom monitored my every move. I felt strangled.

I was temporarily free from Cappy, yes. But the invisible cage around me around me was suffocating.

My life remained like that for several months until my mom felt comfortable enough to add the next atrocity to my already dreadful life. That's right, you guessed it. She allowed the devil back into our home.

I came home one day, and Cappy's black ass was sitting on the couch with his feet up on the coffee table like he was the fucking man.

"'Mika, baby," mom said, "This is my house and I'm tired of the government trying to tell me what to do in my house or who can come into my house. I promise you that things are gonna be hell for you if you bring any trouble into my house. Cappy is staying here and that's that. If it wasn't for you we would already be married and we'd already be in the process of getting my green card."

"Well, that's your choice, Mom," I said. "His time is coming soon anyway. But it's gonna come a lot faster if he comes anywhere near me. You remember what I said? There won't be any groom for the wedding if his ass is buried six feet underground."

"'Mika... you apologize to Cappy right now," Mom said to my back since I was running up the stairs and going to my room. It had been a while since I cried but I allowed myself quite a few tears that day. I was back to living a hell on earth.

A year went by with those living arrangements, with a private investigator following me around school, with Mom dropping me off and picking me up everywhere I went, and with Cappy staring at me like he was gonna pounce the first chance he got.

I talked to Miss Becky from time to time, and she always reminded me to stay strong—which I did. My grades were amazing. I was on the honor roll, making mostly A's with a couple B's here and there. I was even on the debating team. With the injustices I faced from the justice system, I wanted to go to college and then to law school.

But then, those things just weren't in the cards for me.

One day, Cappy had come home and immediately started pitching a bitch about how dirty the house was. My mom had gone to the store to buy laundry detergent and the clothes she had been sorting were strewn all over the kitchen floor.

"Where's your mom?" he barked. I don't know why he thought I'd answer. I never spoke to him, ever, after he'd started abusing me.

"You are such a smart-ass little bitch! I work my ass off taking care of this household and this is the thanks I get?"

I rolled my eyes. Truth be told, even though my dad was arrested for being a kingpin, my mom got a thousand dollars a month from him. He set up an account just in case he ever got locked up. He wanted to make sure that there was enough money to take care of me until I turned nineteen.

"Then," Dad used to say jokingly, "You're on you own." Well, I was already on my own even though I wasn't yet nineteen. I already had to be as smart as any adult.

When Cappy took off his gun belt and uniform and draped them across the chair, I set my expression to show him that I wasn't going to fight back that day.

"Why don't you let me get a little bit while I'm on my lunch? I always love a nooner."

I didn't comment.

"Let's go the bedroom, though," he said. "I don't want the neighbors getting nosy. They would never understand our love."

I almost puked, but I followed him up the stairs to my mother's bedroom anyway.

I followed him into the room and when he was completely naked, I backed away.

"I gotta pee," I said and slyly walked out the room.

"Fuck, Tamika!" he yelled after me. "Hurry up!"

Trust me. I am hurrying, I remember thinking. And that's when Tammy took over.

That day, the upstairs toilet was not working well and Cappy knew I'd have to run downstairs and use the one near the kitchen instead.

Tammy rushed past the bathroom and ran into the kitchen. She tried to be as quiet as possible but Tamika was crying so hard that it was difficult to stop sniffling. She didn't want Cappy to hear the crying.

She grabbed the gun from his belt, making sure to remove the safety, then headed back upstairs.

This is one nigga who's gonna get what he deserves, Tammy thought.

Cappy was laying on my mom's bed, butt naked, with his big, black dick sticking straight in the air.

"You won't be needing that thing today," Tammy said, as she aimed the gun at Cappy.

"Bitch, what the fuck is you doin'?" Cappy asked. "Stop

playin' games and come over here to Poppy."

"Oh, nobody's playing any games," Tammy said. "I'm your judge, jury and prosecution. And on the charge of child molestation, I find you guilty..."

"Child, I told you I'm not playin' wit' you," Cappy said.

"On the charges of evidence tampering and malicious persecution, I find you guilty," Tammy said.

"You really think I'm playin' wit' you?" Cappy asked as he sat up and leaned against the headboard.

"On the charges of assault, battery and just being a plain old monster, I find you guilty as charged, motherfucker," Tammy snapped angrily.

"That's it," Cappy said, jumping his naked ass out the bed and coming towards Tammy and me.

Bang.

"That's what?" Tammy asked after shooting Cappy in the left kneecap. "That's what, motherfucker?"

"Bitch, is you crazy?" Cappy asked. "You have to call an ambulance." He rubbed his leg and looked like he was in intense pain. That made Tammy happy.

"I ain't got to do shit!" Tammy snapped.

"I'm sitting here bleeding to death," Cappy yelled. "Do you hear me? I'm fucking bleeding to death!"

Tammy ignored Cappy. She didn't care if he bled to death or not.

Cappy grunted as he lifted himself off his damaged knee

and lunged at us.

Bang! Bang! Bang!

Tammy shot Cappy three more times, all in the groin area. One of the bullets neatly tore his big black dick right the fuck off. Tammy smiled as she watched it fly across the room.

The nigga got what he deserved.

Afterwards, Tammy ran into my room and grabbed my camera. She took pictures of Cappy's naked body for evidence then ran downstairs and took pictures of the clothing he had taken off and tossed on the kitchen floor.

She knew she was racing against time. Cappy's partner was due to show up at minute. But once she'd finished gathering all the evidence she thought we needed, she left me.

I was alone and scared and didn't know what to do next. I sat on the kitchen floor, crouched in the corner with my knees drawn into my chest, praying that God would forgive me for my part in what Tammy had just done to Cappy.

I remained there in a trance-like state for a long while. Then suddenly, the kitchen door swung open. Mom had returned from the store and she brought Cappy's partner in with her.

She yelled for Cappy. His partner yelled, too. But I just sat there silently on the floor for a long while.

"Why are Cappy's clothes on the floor?" Mom asked.

"I know I heard gun shots," Cappy's partner stated emphatically.

I remained still, trying to understand what had just happened. I didn't say a word. Then Mom grabbed me and started shaking me.

"Girl, what the hell is wrong with you?" she snapped. "What just happened in my house?"

I sighed and summoned the strength to state the facts.

"Cappy tried to rape me again," I said before she cut me off.

"Rape you?"

"Yes," I said, crying. "He tried to rape me again but this time Tammy shot him."

"Girl, you better stop playing with me," Mom yelled. "Where's Cappy? And who the fuck is Tammy?"

"Tammy is my friend," I said emotionlessly. "She protects me. She protected me from Cappy."

"Bitch, nothing better not be wrong with Cappy," my mom shouted as she smacked me across the face. "I ain't your little girlfriend. I'm your mother. So don't fucking play games with me. What the hell happened in my house and where is Cappy?"

"I'm not playing, Mom," I said through teary hiccups, guarding my face with my arms against another slap. "Cappy tried to rape me again. You already know that he's been raping me for a while."

Mom balled up her fist and punched me on my forearm. It immediately started pulsating and hurting like hell. I was glad that she hit my arm instead of my face. If I hadn't protected myself, I would have had a black eye.

"Bitch, Cappy ain't thinking about you!" she screamed. "I don't know why you're always trying to bring me trouble. He's been nothing but good to you. You need to just give him a break and start treating him better. Every time he reaches out to you, you pull away."

"That's because he only reaches out to her when he's trying to feel her up."

I heard my voice, but I knew it wasn't me speaking. Tammy was back.

"Bitch, you ain't gonna talk bad about Cappy like that!" Mom snapped. "You take it back!"

She started punching again, aiming to get to my face. "I said take it the fuck back!"

"No, Bitch, you get back!" Tammy shouted as she kicked my mother off me.

Mom fell back onto the kitchen table with a crazed look on her face.

"You're gonna kick me, Tamika?" she asked eerily.

"You need to just leave her alone," Tammy said. "Since you couldn't protect her from him, I'm here to protect her from everybody."

Mom squared up. Tammy squared up. And I just stood there horrified, not knowing what was about to go down.

"Katrina! Oh my God!" Cappy's partner shouted. I heard loud footsteps pounding their way down the stairs. I had forgotten all about him. "Cappy's laying on the floor, butt naked with bullet wounds! It looks like he was shot execution-style."

"He's butt naked because he was going to rape Tamika again," Tammy snapped. "And your trifling ass was right outside in the car knowing that he was about to take away more of her innocence," she said to his partner.

"You shut the fuck up, you smart little bitch!" Cappy's partner shouted.

"Oh no! Cappy!!" My mother screamed as she dashed out of the kitchen and up the stairs. From the kitchen, I heard her wailing, "Oh no! Cappy! You have to wake up, baby. Wake up, baby! Please, please get up. Get up, Cappy! Get up. You have to get up!"

I felt sick inside. My mother was completely distraught over a man who'd been raping her daughter for years. He had put both me and her through hell yet she acted like he was the second coming of Christ.

Mom stayed upstairs for what seemed like an eternity. All the while, Cappy's partner was on his radio calling for back-up and medical assistance.

"Repeat, officer down!" he shouted frantically into his radio. "I need back-up immediately. I also need an ambulance equipped to deal with multiple gunshot wounds."

Between my mother's screams upstairs and Cappy's partner shouting into the radio downstairs, I couldn't think. And quickly, things got even crazier.

"No! No! No!" Mom screamed again as she ran down the stairs. "You've ruined everything!" she screamed at me as she raced towards me. "Why'd you have to kill Cappy? I loved him. I love him so much." She swung at me wildly as she professed her love for my rapist.

Tammy couldn't take it. She swung at Mom and connected. Mom's mouth quickly started to puff up.

"Bitch, you should be ashamed of yourself!" Tammy scolded. "You are sitting here fucking crying over the man who had been raping your daughter!"

Mom started to cry even harder.

"You're my own flesh and blood and you hit me?" she asked incredulously. "And you shot Cappy? What in the hell has gotten into you, Tamika?"

"Tamika's tired of that beast having his way with her," Tammy said with an attitude. "But we don't have to worry about that anymore now, do we?"

"I hate you!" Mom snarled as she ran towards us.

She grabbed me around my neck and started to choke me.

Tammy tried to fight her off but Cappy's partner grabbed us both so that Mom could do as she pleased with us.

Between Cappy and my mom, Tammy and I got roughed up pretty badly before the ambulance and the police back-up arrived. By the time I was roughly thrown into the back of the police car with my hands cuffed behind me, I had bruises all over my body and I could barely breathe.

I was under arrest but I was glad that the cops showed up when they did or I would have been dead, too.

Tammy had intended that the photos would show that Cappy's attack on Tamika had been premeditated. But instead, the prosecutor claimed the photos proved that Cappy's murder had been premeditated. We thought we had an open and shut case. Apparently not.

"How could this murder not have been planned?" the prosecutor asked. "When the gun was removed from the decedent's clothes—which were downstairs—the defendant had every opportunity to escape the premises. The decedent was upstairs without a stitch on yet the defendant didn't escape. She didn't want to. She wanted to enact justice because she felt that the system had failed her. Maybe it did. But we are still not allowed to take matters into our own hands. Eventually justice prevails. Tamika just had to wait a little longer and it would've prevailed in her case."

Not! Justice never prevailed in my case—despite all of

the evidence that my lawyer presented, including the expert testimony of Dr. Barnaby who told the court that I'd been diagnosed as a schizophrenic—despite the fact that Cappy ignored the restraining order and came within one hundred feet of me—despite everything I'd already been through, I was found guilty of second degree manslaughter and sentenced to ten years in prison.

BOOK THREE

In The Game

CHAPTER ELEVEN

Prison

Age 20

Hi Dad,

I hope this letter finds you in good health. It has taken me a long while to write to you and I hope you understand that I always wanted to. But I wasn't sure if you wanted to hear from me. I wasn't even sure where you were.

Before I was sent away, I snuck around mom's room and found this address. She obviously didn't want me to have it or she would have given it to me a long time ago. I kept it hidden in my room for a long time. I even memorized it. I knew someday I would have to write. That day has come.

I'm certain that you're doing a lot better than I am. I'm also certain that you have learned through the grapevine what has happened to me. I know you must be doing better than I am. You're on the outside, free. I am locked up in this awful prison, trying to stay out of trouble and be a model prisoner. It is really tough here. Life is a mother when you're stuck up in here. But of course you know that.

I saw some of the video footage from your arrival back to Jamaica a few years ago. I begged to see more and Ms. Betty from the shelter was able to get helpe me. She was such a sweetheart. I don't know what I would've done without her.

You looked so debonair in the video. You are so handsome. And you look like the pillar of strength. It's no wonder that everyone in sight was sucking up to you. Even a blind man could see how much power and respect you commanded. From dignitaries even! Your name and reputation are truly legendary.

Respect like that must have been hard earned. I know it didn't come lightly. That's the kind of respect I need, and I'm willing to work just as hard as you did to get it. I'm willing to work even harder.

It's funny. When I was doing everything that I was supposed to be doing, all the world and the system did was take advantage of me. It seemed like people came into my life just to take something from me they didn't deserve.

I earned good grades in school, and I tried to be the perfect daughter. But no one recognized my efforts after you got locked up. No one really cared about me. Mom had her head stuck so far up Cappy's butt that she wasn't even aware that I still existed. I felt so alone.

I was a good girl. But I was left alone and ignored. I was just a little girl. Who was going to listen to me? The biggest mistake I made was not running as away soon as I realized that Mom was going to let Cappy stay around for good. With all of his touching and feeling and shit, I don't know why I didn't realize sooner that things would escalate. Maybe I was just too much of a little girl. I hope you don't blame me

I did everything I was supposed to do, took every advantage that was presented to me, yet the system didn't protect me. Looking out for me was the last thing the system did! I now know that I have to look out for myself.

That's why I want to follow in your footsteps. I need the same type of respect that you got on the streets. I need for people to look at me and feel the same fear they felt when they looked at you. Maybe if people gave any thought about the consequences of their actions, some of the things that happened to me would never have happened. And I want to guarantee that none of that type of stuff happens to me again.

I'm sure you want me to be a lawyer or a doctor or something big and fancy. But we don't choose the paths in life that are set for us. We just follow them, wherever they lead.

I don't complain anymore about any of the things that happened to me. All I try to do is learn from my experiences and use them to make me stronger. Pardon my French, Dad, but I plan to be the strongest bitch out there on the streets. And before it's all over, people are gonna look at me with the same respect they had for you.

Your legacy is already set in stone. I want my legacy to follow yours.

I love you dad,
Tamika

After writing the letter, I sealed it and put it in the mailboz just outside the library. It felt good to finally write to my dad and tell him my plans. Then I went back into the library to find every book I could that would help me hold my own out on the streets.

I found myself reading about crime legends in New York, Miami, even Philadelphia. I learned about cliques like the Junior Black Mafia in Philadelphia to the Cuban crews of Miami that prompted Hollywood to produce the movie *Scarface*. But no matter how diverse the situations were, they all had one thing in common — at the top was somebody that got the utmost respect. Their crews looked up to them and relied on them — no matter what! The leader always held things down in the same way that my father did and in the same way that I aspired to hold things down once I got the chance.

"Bitch, you ain't no fucking princess! You ain't special," Sarah Talbert shouted. "You're just a fucking criminal like the rest of us. And when you get out of here, you ain't gonna have a pot to piss in just like the rest of us. So what you need to do is stop hyping yourself up and thinking that you sit on the top of a totem pole or something. Bring your ass back down off that cloud and land in the gutter with the rest of us."

Sarah Talbert was the type of woman who acted like she had been defeated by life. I don't have any idea what happened to her. But she acted like nobody had been through more than she had been.

Sarah was about five feet nine with a really striking figure that she went out of her way to hide. Her skin was flawless and her features would have made her one of the most beautiful woman in the world if she allowed them to, which she didn't. Sarah was a lesbian to the core and she was too butch to even think about wanting to look beautiful.

Sarah was the type of woman who believed if she looked too good other woman would perceive her to be soft. So she chose to do her damnedest to hide the stunning looks that God gave her. And while she tried to hide her good looks, she also adopted an indifferent attitude to ensure that no one found a speck of internal beauty inside her either. All Sarah wanted was for the world to think that she was rotten to the core so they'd fear her.

And speaking of fear, since Sarah stepped to me the way she just did, I couldn't just let it ride. I had just told my dad that I wanted the same type of respect he got so I couldn't start by getting a reputation in prison as the type of person who would let some chick back her into a corner. I couldn't let anyone think that I was gonna let somebody say what they damned well pleased to me.

Although I wasn't planning for things to happen so fast, my ascension to the top of the hustle game had to start right there in prison. I wanted the reverberations of how I handled myself in prison to be heard throughout New York City. So, regrettably for Sarah, she was put on display. She was a pawn that would be knocked over in my chess game. If only she would have kept her dumb-ass mouth shut! But she didn't.

I sashayed over to Sarah and started punching her repeatedly in her gorgeous face.

"You have something to say to me, Sarah?" I asked as I delivered each blow. "Do you feel like you need to get in my business?"

Everyone was stunned. No one could believe that the new girl, the quiet girl that had been there for months, would lay the smack-down on the biggest bully in the correctional facility. But that's what I did. If they knew who I was, they wouldn't have doubted me in the first place. I had a destiny to fulfilland I was staking my claim.

After I finish beating Sarah down, I looked around at the few women who were staring in awe at me and made a pronouncement.

"Just because I haven't fucked with anybody in here doesn't mean I'm soft. If y'all don't know who Marley is, you're about to find. I'm his little girl. And, like father like daughter, nobody better disrespect me again. Y'all would be better off to leave my name out of your mouths and my business out of your minds."

I turned and walked away amidst stares and whispers.

"That can't be Marley's daughter, can it? Is she the one who killed that bastard-ass cop?"

"Yeah, I think she is."

My new-found fans chattered as I walked back to my cell. I let the facts sink into their heads to marinate in their minds. By the time I got out of prison, I knew that everyone on the streets would have something to say about Tamika.

CHAPTER TWELVE

Tamika at Bedford Hills Correctional Facility

"Fess up, Tamika," barked CO Green. "We know you know something about what happened to Sarah. We know things have never been peachy-keen between you two."

"I don't know what you're talking about, sir," I said.

I knew that I couldn't drop dimes in prison. And I would have been a fool to tell on myself. My only option was to act innocent. That was my story and I stuck to it.

"Do you wanna go in the hole, Tamika?" CO Green asked. "Do you need some time by yourself to think or are you gonna help us out?"

"Do what you have to do, sir," I said. "I already told you that I don't have any idea what happened so I don't know what else I'm supposed to tell you."

"Just get the fuck out of here then," he barked. "But know that I'm gonna have my eyes on you," he said, pointing his fingers at his eyes. "You ain't gonna be able to do shit around here without me knowing about it."

I walked back through the corridors of the Bedford Hills Correctional Facility feeling like I'd just won a small battle.

Too many people opened their mouths when dealing with law enforcement personnel when they didn't have to. If the man had something on you, he didn't need to come at you on a fishing expedition. He'd just put whatever proof he had out there and flaunt it in your face, trying to get you to turn on someone to save yourself. But if he said he knew that you were involved, the reality was that he didn't know exactly what it was. All you had to do was stand your ground, remain calm, and you'd walk away from the situation totally unscathed.

That was what I did. But as far as the inmates were concerned, that was a different story. I knew Sarah had loyal followers and they might come at me to see if I was as strong as I appeared to be.

Truth be told, I hadn't attempted to bond with anyone in prison. I was on the same island I had created for myself long ago. I was isolated but primed for infiltration if someone tried to reach me. But I didn't have anyone at my back.

It may not have been the best situation to be in at Bedford Hills. The prison housed some hardened women. There were arsonists, drug dealers, murderers and worse. Every woman had a story, too. Something had drastically gone wrong in all of their lives before they got to prison. And so, they were all just as fucked up in the head as I had been. In that regard, I didn't have an advantage over any of them. But I did feel like I had an advantage as far as my heart was concerned. I was not afraid of anybody but myself. I just hoped I didn't have too much courage. I didn't want overconfidence to be the thing that brought me down.

As sat on my cot and wondered if I went too far with Sarah, Sally Strothers showed up outside my cell. Sally was diminutive but a ball of fire. She'd been known to put the largest women in check when she had to. But she was also known for her kind heart and passion.

Sally was the only person who'd been able to get to one of the most famous prisoners in this institution, Sharon Richardson. Sharon Richardson was locked up for the murd- of her boyfriend. She wasn't accused of killing him but was sentenced because she was present when it happened and was suspected to have been instrumental in the planning of his killing.

Like me, Sharon Richardson was physically, sexually, and emotionally abused by the person she was in jail for killing. So were several other women in that institution, all betrayed by the system. We were bitter and had large oceans to cross before mending our psychological wounds. But i wasn't sure if I was ready for Sally. I was about saving my pretty black ass and making it out of prison alive.

"Do you have a minute, Tamika?" Sally askd.

"Yeah," I said, "But my head is kind of messed up right now. I have a lot to think about."

"I guess so," Sally said. "Coming at Sarah like that. You know she thinks she's the godmother."

I looked at Sally like she was trying to set me up.

"Relax," she assured me, "I'm not trying to get all up in your business though I am trying to get in your business. Really, all I'm just trying to do is help you. Whether you know it or not, you need help right now. Sarah and her people are not just gonna sit back and take what happened to her."

"Actually, I was pondering that just now," I confessed.

"Well, I don't know what to tell you to say to her or her people," Sally said, "but I hope you're smarter in future dealings with her. You can't allow your temper get the best of you."

"True, but I can't just let those chicks disrespect me either, calling me a bitch."

"What does it really mean to be called a bitch?" Sally asked. "I mean, how does it hurt, really?"

"It's not always about hurt," I replied. "Sometimes it's about respect. My mom's so-called boyfriend disrespected me repeatedly, calling me names. It got to a point that I started to wonder if he even knew my real name. I refuse to let anyone make me feel the way he did ever again."

"So hearing someone call you names brings back painful memories?" Sally asked.

"Hell, yeah!" I said.

"Well think about this," Sally said, "all of the things he did to you eventually made you react in a way that got you here. So, even though he paid for what he did to you, in a way he still won because you're here. Don't let him keep winning, Tamika. If someone calls you a bitch, so what? How many famous women embrace being called a bitch? Look at Li'l Kim, look at Trina. I'm not saying that you have to embrace it but you shouldn't let the word get you into deep water. You shouldn't let being called a bitch back you into a corner and force you to make bad choices. At the end of the day, you know who you are. And you know who the people who talk about you are. Trust me, on their best day they couldn't be better than you if you were having your worst day. So why even sweat them? Just be proud that they're probably coming at you because they want to be like you. Hell, some of them probably wish they could be you. Don't let them bring you down. If they say you're a bitch, show them that you're the best bitch there is."

"I hear you but it's not that easy," I said even though I knew that Sally was right.

"I'm not expecting an overnight transformation," Sally said, "but I know you don't deserve to be here. And I want you to walk out of here one hundred percent cool. I want you to be a better person leaving than you were coming in."

"How often does that happen?" I asked sarcastically but not in a way that's too smart.

"It doesn't happen often," Sally replied. "But then, people like you don't come in here that often. I used to go through the ringer talking to Sharon because she's the same type of victim you are. But look at her now. She's lifted herself up despite her circumstances, despite her mishaps. You have the opportunity to use everything that has happened to you to build your character. What doesn't kill you only makes you stronger, right? Don't allow these women in here to bring you down. The bottom line is that you have to be smart enough to safely walk through those prison gates when your time comes."

"When is it gonna be your time to get out of here?" I asked.

"Nevruary."

"Never?" I asked. "You're never getting out of here? Damn. What did you do?"

"Nothing."

"Damn. You need the same thing then that every other bitch in here does," I said.

Sally hugged me and smiled, letting me know that she knew I understand what she was saying.

"I'll try to smooth things out with Sarah and her clique,"

Sally promised. "But you're gonna have to try to control your temper."

"I will," I said. "And if people want me to be a bitch, I'll be the best bitch that I can. But you"re right. I'm not gonna let the memory of Cappy's black ass bring me down. He's done enough to me already."

That was the first of many conversations I had with Sally. And I can't tell you how many times she saved my ass. I can't tell you how many times I snapped and lost it.

Luckily for me, the no-snitching code, prevalent on every street corner in urban America, also held true in prison. I was sure the prison brass knew that I had done many things but nothing could be proven. No one ever turned me in.

They say God protects babies and fools. He must have been protecting me as well because I had been a humongous fool during my time in prison. But, at the same time, I was preparing myself for life when I got out. I'd been building a reputation that made people look at me in awe just like they looked at my father.

Dad told me in his letters that he had heard rumors about me on the streets. Undoubtedly, he heard them from the relatives of the women I was locked down with. So as dumb as I had been acting, I began to realize that I was reaping the benefits I wanted. But I was totally floored by what I had to do to maintian. Surprise after surprise.

A week before my release, after lights out, I was relaxing in my bed, reading, when a shadow appeared outside my cell. When I looked up, I saw Sarah standing there with CO Green.

"You didn't think you were just gonna waltz out of here without paying for what you did, did you?"

His yellow teeth are highly visible in the din light as he smiling widely. I wasn't sure why Sarah was there, though. She couldn't take me on before by herself so I figured she brought back-up this time.

"What's this about, Green?"

"Oh, I you knoe what it's about," he said. "Payback's a bitch. But it's a necessary evil. And your ass is not getting out of here until Sarah gets her payback for what you did to her."

"So, you think that Sarah can take me?" I asked, rolling my eyes.

"That's what this is all about," Sarah said. "I have every intention in the world to take you."

"I just want to stand out here and watch you bitches," CO Green said with his a smile.

Green unlocked my cell and closed locked it after Sarah came in. As she got closer to my bed, I realized that for once she doesn't look quite so butch. Her beauty is stunning.

"What's this about, Sarah?" I asked softly so that CO Green couldn't hear me.

"No one has ever handled me like that before, Tamika," Sarah said, barely above a whisper. "And honestly, the way you handled me turned me the fuck on. Yeah, you beat me in a fair fight. But you're not naïve enough to believe that everything just went away. I'm sure you think that Sally had soemthing to do with people staying out of your way after we got into it. But hell no! I kept everyone off your ass. they didn't retaliate on my behalf and mess you up because I wanted you just as fine as you always are when I get my payback. I didn't want nobody messing up that pretty face or that sexy body of yours. I gave up my revenge so I can have this night. Now I want to collect. It's time for you to pay your debt."

"Pay my debt? But how, Sarah?" I asked. But I already had an idea, knowing the type of chick she was.

Without a word, Sarah lifted her long t-shirt and pulled it over her head. Underneath, she was butt-ass naked but standing in front of me as confident as I'd ever seen her.

Sarah's titties put mine to shame. They were huge but firm. They looked very soft and natural, though.

Her waist was as slim as they come. She looked like she could fit into a size two if her waist had anything to say about it. But her thick thighs and monster ass were doing all the talking.

She had also put on some make-up and looked as beautiful any actress I'd ever seen on television or in the movies.

At least she came in here correct, I thought as she sat

down next to me on my cot.

It wasn't my thing but I did hear what Sarah was saying. No matter how long it took, I knew a comeback was in store for me.

As I looked at Sarah, I knew that all wanted from me was to fulfill some type of sexual fantasy she had in her head. Obviously, she wasn't threatening me. She came at me peacefully. And she looked so hot. But I had to lay down the rule.

"I'm not eating your pussy, Sarah," I said. "I never have and I have no plans of doing that shit now."

"You don't have to, baby," Sarah said while pulling closer and kissing me on my neck. "Really, I'm just dying to taste you. But if you can manage it, I love to have my titties sucked. And I wouldn't be mad at you if you fucked me with your fingers."

To be honest, I wanted to investigate Sarah's titties. I wanted to feel them and caress and massage them. I wanted to suck on them.

With my mind at ease, knowing that she didn't want me to eat her pussy, I was able to relax. I allowed her to take off my clothes and seduce me by kissing and licking me all over.

When the two of us were snuggling together totally naked, Sarah kissed me on my mouth. Gay shit was not my thing but Sarah was so beautiful. And she was so sweet that I would have felt guilty to not allow her her fantasy as passionately and as erotically as she had imagined it.

Her tongue and lips were soft and sweet. She kissed my lips and wrapped her tongue around my tongue with the same care that she used to explore the rest of my body with her hands. I felt myself getting moist between my legs. I felt myself being turned on by the way she touched me.

As she started placing her kisses on my neck and chest, I softly massaged her hair and looked her straight in the eyes.

Never in a million years would I have imagined that we would do what we were then doing, especially after I punched her in the face! But as I looked at it, I realized I was a fool. She was so beautiful, amazingly beautiful. And my body was amazed at how she is at made me feel good.

By the time Sarah was fully into eating my pussy, I was squirming and moaning. I looked outside my cell and noticed that CO Green had his dick out and was playing with himself as he watched us. He was some type of a pervert. And he was trifling as hell, too.

As I muffled my screams as much as I could so no one heard my orgasm, I heard him having his own orgasm. I turned my head and saw his semen shoot out on the floor.

He didn't even have the decency to wipe it up. He didn't wipe off his hands either. He kept looking at us, wondering what we do next.

I tried to get Green out of my head so I planted a kiss on Sarah's lips. She deserved a kiss for making me tremble like that.

I fulfilled my desire to examine her breasts by massaging them as we continue to kiss. They were as soft and luscious as I had imagined.

"Kiss them, baby," Sarah begged me.

Her sweet talk turned me on so much. I didn't think it was possible. It was as if she'd had a complete metamorphosis in character. I couldn't believe how open she was to me. I sort of felt honored that she allowed me to see that side of her that I was sure very few people got the chance to see.

I kissed Sarah's neck on my way to what I really wanted to kiss on. At that moment, I remember that all I wanted was to suck on her breasts.

Her neck tasted as sweet as her lips. I was drawn to her scent.

"Let me leave you a little something to remember me by," I said as I sucked on her neck hard. "I want you to be able to look in the mirror and relive this fantasy. In fact, you should take a picture to remember me by."

Talking to Sarah seductively had the desired effect on her I hope for. She started to writhe uncontrollably on the cot and her movements became even more pronounced as I started to suck on and rub her nipples.

I didn't know where I got the urge or if I was just caught up in the moment but I reached down between her legs and slipped my fingers into her wetness. She moaned loudly as soon as I touched her.

"Oh yes, baby, fuck me with your fingers," she begged.

I obliged her and continued to massage her titties with my free hand.

My mouth and tongue explored every inch of her titties. I licked her nipples a certain way to elicit a response from her. I wanted to know if I was making her feel good. I didn't want it to be just about her nipples though. I wanted to suck hard on the meat of her titties and leave my mark on her. I wanted her to remember the passion. And I guess I wanted to thank her for making my stay in prison better than it would have been if she hadn't been looking out for me.

"Oh yes, baby," Sarah moaned. "Fuck my pussy with your fingers. Get my juices all over your pretty hands."

I knew by the shakiness in her voice that Sarah was about to climax. So I increased the speed in which I thrust my fingers in and out of her pussy and concentrated on licking and sucking her nipples.

"Oh God, Tamika! Oh God!" she said as she arched her back. I felt her warm juices run over my fingers. I felt so proud of myself for taking Sarah where she so desperately needed to go.

Afterwards, she took a few moments to compose herself before laying her head next to mine and snuggling with me.

"You were great, baby," she said before planting a sweet

kiss on my lips. "You were everything I dreamed you'd be."

"You weren't so bad yourself," I said. "I'm not into the things that you're into, but there's nothing wrong with keeping it real. I wasn't turned off at any time while I was kissing on you. Your body has a mesmerizing scent that's ungodly."

"Thanks for saying that, Tamika, but you don't have to butter me up," Sarah said. "I'm just happy you let me go through with this."

"I'm not just buttering you up," I said.

I lifted the hand that I used to finger fuck her and sucked her juices off me. I surprised myself by my action.

"See? You know I'm not into this," I said. "But goddamn you taste sweet! I'm really glad we did this."

Sarah grabbed my head and pulled me to her face and gave me the most passionate kiss that I'd ever had to that point.

"Thank you so much," she said after she broke away. "You don't know what this night meant to me."

"I'm glad I could help you out," I said with a smile.

"Alright you two, break it up," CO Green said. After getting off a couple of times, he started rushing us. "I don't have time to sit here and be a part of your tender moment. I have to get you back into your cell," he said to Sarah.

"Bye, baby," Sarah said before stealing a last kiss.

She stood up and her ass jiggled as she picked up her oversized t-shirt. Her pussy looked very inviting as she bent over.

"Sarah," I called out as she pulled her t-shirt over her head. "Maybe we could continue this another time."

"I would love that," she said.

"But what happens in Bedford stays in Bedford," I said.

"No doubt," Sarah said with a wink and left.

I spent several more nights with Sarah before I left Bedford. I even tasted her sweet pussy and allowed her to taste mine again and again.

Yet none of it would have happened if I didn't think that the code of silence was in effect. A lot of same-sex shit happens in prison and it's forgotten once you walk out the doors. It's a sin to ever open your mouth and tell.

All I knew was that I lost my temper on several occasions under Sarah's watchful eye without repercussions.

And I couldn't be mad at her for giving me orgasms. All in all, Sarah was a really sweet person, just turning on the touch act that when she needed it.

Getting to know her during that week also taught me a couple of lessons about the game. The most important, though, was to always show people the side of you that the streets needed to see. Only extremely close friends should ever be able to see the sweet person inside. And if I followed that reasoning, I would never have to worry about being taken down by a pretender. I learned that from Sarah, the most beautiful chick I'd ever seen.

It was my last night sleeping on a lumpy cot and eating terrible food. I was so excited to be getting out. But I had to write my dad one more time and take care of business with him, too.

Hi Dad,

I hope that this letter finds you in good health. I'm getting out tomorrow and hopefully it won't be too long before I see your handsome face again.

We never really talked about mom. I was afraid to go there, afraid that you would hate me or something. But if I'm going to begin my new life in the streets as strong and as confident as you, then I have to get a few things off my chest.

Mom was a shit to me. She drilled it into my head every single day that you had deserted us. I didn't want to believe her at first, but after a while, I did.

She didn't protect me from Cappy. She refused to believe me. All she dreamed of was becoming a naturalized citizen. Mom is brain-dead sometimes. Cappy was never planning on marrying her Everyone knew it. Sometimes I wish I had told Aunt Toni or somebody what Cappy was doing to me. But every time I thought about it, I realizzed who was going to believe me? You would have. But then if youwere here for me to tell then there wouldn't have been a Cappy around in the first place!

I can't keep living in the past. I know that. What has happened has already happened. But I feel as bad about Mom betraying you as I do about her betraying me. She did both of us dirty, Dad.

I want you to understand that I love you more than anything. I won't disrespect Mom, but I won't go looking for her either. I can't ever mess with her again. She ruined my life. To get back in it, she's going to have to do some serious kissing on my ass and we both know that Mom's not that type of person. She believes she's right even when she's wrong.

It doesn't matter what she thinks, though. I'm sure she thinks I'm wrong for what I did to Cappy.

But later for her. I can't be getting all sensitive now that I'm about to follow in your footsteps. I'm glad that we're back in each other's lives. I've missed you so much. I've missed your knowledge and wisdom. I've missed seeing your handsome smile. I've even missed you letting me get away with everything! The streets are going to be tough on me. But I promise to make you real proud of me.

But I love you for that, too. You've been everything a parent is supposed to be. I'm ashamed for ever having doubted you. I hope that you can find a way to forgive me.

Dad, I love you much.

Your daughter,
Tamika

CHAPTER THIRTEEN

Out

I was in prison for a total of six years. And when I was released, it was with nothing—not a pot to piss in nor a leg to stand on. Justice had been served but I felt like I'd been royally fucked.

I didn't leave prison a dumb-ass, though. I stayed strong like Becky told me to do and continued with my studies.

I got my high school diploma. And even received an online Criminal Justice degree from Princeton University with a minor in Business. I didn't care that people tried to clown me and called my degree artificial. A bachelor's degree from Princeton was still impressive. I knew it would get me a good job even if I had to hand over a sob story about how I got the degree in the first place.

But I had other things on my mind than getting a job.

While I was locked down, I did a lot of research about my

dad. I never would have imagined that he was ballin' the way he was.

My dad wasn't even forty years old but he'd managed in twenty-five years to build a drug cartel that employed over a hundred people and netted hundreds of millions of dollars a year. And if it wasn't for lying-ass Cappy, he would never have been caught.

So I got to thinking that maybe hustlin' was in my blood. I decided that when I got out, I was gonna step out into the game and learn the things my dad had mastered.

It was totally frustrating trying to get put on and having everybody turn me away. The first question was always, "Ain't you Marley's seed?" When I told them I was, they froze up like a deer caught in the headlights. Then they walked away mumbling something about how they ain't fuckin' wit' me.

I didn't get it. Who wouldn't want the daughter of one of the greatest criminal minds ever to be on their squad? I had to take after my dad in some kind of way, didn't I?

I really didn't know what the fuck was going on but something had to pop off sooner or later. Shit was getting really tight for me. I was running low on the money I had stashed away from the part-time job Miss Becky helped me get before I left the shelter. *Pretty soon*, I thought, *I may have to resort to sticking motherfuckers up if I don't catch a break.*

The break I'd been hoping for finally fell in my lap.

One day, this tall, lanky, weird-looking dude named Rodman approached me. I heard he got his nickname because physically he was supposed to resemble the ex-basketball player. But I didn't see it.

Rodman had a little crew, nothing major, but people in his camp made a couple dollars. I wouldn't be flashy if he put me down. But at least I'd be OK until something better came along.

"I hear you need some work," Rodman said to me, bowing down when he reached me.

"What's all that?" I asked.

"I thought that's the way you're supposed to address royalty," Rodman replied.

"Shit, don't nothing feel royal about my broke ass right about now!"

"I can say a lot of things about that ass, ma," he said, "but I would never call it broke."

He thought he was being charming and flirtatious but I was offended.

"Listen up, playboy," I said, irked but still respectful. "I'm not cool wit' all those sexual innuendos and shit like that. I'm ready to get my grind on but you can best believe that I'm just trying to do business—nothing else."

"My bad, ma," he said. "I ain't mean nothing by it. You're just cute, that's all."

"Well, cute ain't gettin' me no fucking money so I ain't beat for nobody recognizing that I'm cute. I just need motherfuckers to recognize that I'm trying to be about my paper."

I was extremely hard on Rodman but I really didn't blame him for the compliment. After all the years of physical fitness I did when I was down had been kind to me.

My skin had always been flawlessly beautiful. And my body was always decent, too. I might have been a little flabby at one time. But my body changed from mundane to insane in jail, and my ass would have J-Lo asking me for exercise tips. I'm a full C-cup but if I stopped working out, they'd go back to D's like they used to be.

I'm most proud of my stomach. It is the tightest six-pack you'd ever want to see. And my leg are stunning. Although I'm muscle bound, I didn't overdo it like a body builder. I still looked sexy as all hell. Any man would have reacted to me the way Rodman did. But I had to put his ass in check. I didn't want any complications. I had plans on being big time, and I wasn't gonna let some nigga that wasn't even cute fuck it up for me because he got a hard-on looking at me.

"So, Miss Jefferson," Rodman said.

"Call me Tammy," I said quickly.

"OK, Tammy. Are you gonna dead my comments so we can get at this paper or have you decided that you ain't fucking wit' a nigga like me because of it."

"I'm listening, Rodman," I said, "but you haven't said

much yet."

"OK. I respect that," he said, smiling. "You want me to get to the point. Ain't nothing wrong wit' gettin' right down to business and shit."

"Rodman, I'm growing gray hairs," I said sarcastically.

"Well, check this out," he said. "If I give you this pack of hydro that's worth about twelve hundred bagged up, and if you were able to get rid of it, you would get to keep five and give me seven. That should help you to get your feet wet and let me see if you're ready for bigger and better things."

"Oh, I'm definitely ready for bigger and better things," I said, smiling inside. "So when is all of this going down?"

"Once you agree to my one condition," he said, looking serious as all hell. "Once you look me in the eye and promise me that you'll put in a good word for me with your old man—let him know that I looked out for you when no one else would."

"That doesn't seem so hard," I said.

"Well then, promise me," he demanded.

"Chill out," I said. "It's not that serious."

"Tammy, promise me," he said again.

"OK, nigga. Damn!" I said, getting irked. "I promise you. The next time I talk to my dad I'll let him know. Don't catch a fucking hissy fit."

Rodman ignored me and walked off. A few minutes later, another dude rode by and threw a small sack out the window.

It landed near my feet. I was about to be officially indoctrinated into my dad's game. And all I had to do was sell some weed, I mean, hydro.

CHAPTER FOURTEEN

Big Surprise

Hi Tamika,

As I promised myself, I'm writing you again today. By now you should have received my first letter. And I should be expecting to receive your first letter soon, too.

I'm sure that when I get it you will apologize for being an asshole to your dad and you'll be asking for my forgiveness. But that won't be necessary. I'm gonna always be your dad and believe it or not, I do understand how much pressure you were under.

I've already reached out to the guards and other people at the prison. They will keep tabs on you and I'll know how you are at all times.

They've been feeling you so you have been

successful earning your stripes. In the game, people will resent you because of whose daughter you are.

I should have done more to ensure that you were ok. I can't figure out for the life of me why I didn't put one of my best men on it.

I never trusted Katrina before when it came to you. She was so jealous of you and me! I don't know what the hell I was thinking.

I am a big enough man, though, to apologize to you. I should have protected you better. I owed you that much and I let you down. I hope you know that I will never let you down again.

Love, Dad

Reading those words from my dad made me feel so good. He really did respect me as a person, something my mom had never done.

And he's been true to his word. Even though I'm out of prison, he knew where to send the letter. So he does have people watching out for me.

I can't speak for other women, but think a woman needs to have a good relationship with her father. That love will always stop her in her tracks and make her think. She'll always be worried about what he'll think of her.

My main concern was making him proud of me and erasing all the bad stuff in my past in the process.

It took me a lot longer to sell the weed than I wanted it to. Three days had passed and it wasn't even halfway gone. Rodman tried to be supportive in his dumb-ass way. Still and all, some of his comments annoyed me so much I thought I might have to cut his tongue out one day.

"It's not that hard, Tammy. Niggas are smoking weed like it's going out of style. And you ain't got no bullshit. You got dro. That should make it even easier."

"I ain't a fucking idiot, Rodman," I said, sounding as irritated as I felt. "I know niggas are smokin' the shit. I just don't know where those niggas are at."

"Well if you stop trying to be so fucking serious all the time then maybe some shit will just come to you," he said.

I rolled my eyes.

"Nah, I'm for real," he continued. "You have to go to a couple parties. Niggas be blazing that shit up outside the parties on the sidewalk, in the rides, and sometimes right in the fucking party. And wit' your sexy ass, I'm sure you can get a motherfucker's attention. Then when the nigga try to holla that's when you sell his ass some weed. It ain't hard, Tammy. Use what you got to get what you want."

"Do you wanna fuck me or summin', Rodman?" I asked,

heated. "Because you keep talkin' real slick and saying all this pretty shit even though I already told you that it bothers me. That's like sexual harassment."

"I'm just trying to be real wit' you, Tammy," he said. "Shit, this is the streets. You use whatever fucking thing you can that gives you an advantage. And I ain't sayin' that I'm trying to fuck you just 'cuz I tell you to use your good looks to your advantage."

"Nigga, please. If I offered you some of this pussy you'd be breaking your neck to get to it," I teased.

"And what nigga wouldn't, Tammy? You're hot. But it's not about trying to fuck you right now."

"You see, nigga, that's where your problem is," I told him. "It should never be about trying to fuck me. Not just right now. Not now, not ever."

"I feel you on that," he said, "but you are missing my point. All I'm trying to say is that you should get out there and mingle a little. I'm not telling you to be a party animal. Just mingle a little. Go out. Let niggas see your face. Then sell the niggas you feel comfortable with your product. It'll be like taking candy from a baby. All you have to do is believe it then you can achieve it."

"Save the motherfucking pep talk, Rodman. I'm too old for that shit to help me now. Just tell me where the party's at and I'll give your way a try. But don't be looking at my ass if I put on some shit and you decide to show up." I continued to tease. "I'll be getting dressed for the motherfuckers that spend money, not for you."

"Oh, I'm spending, girl. I'm definitely spending," he said, licking his lips.

I ignored the comment that took me back to when I was younger, when the white man named John paid me to have sex with him. Men are some nasty motherfuckers and will always try to buy some ass in a heartbeat.

I wasn't thinking about fucking anyone at all. But still, it was good to know I had Rodman in my back pocket. But he wouldn't be necessary. I had to get home and throw on some sexy clothes. I was gonna sell out of my shit.

I went home and took a long, hot shower. Then I threw on a pair of Baby Phat jeans that were made to show off my butt cleavage and a cropped and frayed camouflage Baby Phat wife beater. I wanted people to get a good look at my sexy waist and stomach as well as my ass. I wanted to have them drooling. I topped off my look off with a pair of black Timberlands that I flipped to show off the camouflage lining. I looked dead sexy.

I pulled my hair back into one long, simple ponytail before taking a good look at my face in the mirror. It looked too flawless to mess up with makeup but I did put on a little lip gloss just to remind the niggas that I was a woman.

Before I headed out, I sprayed on some True Star perfume

in a few strategic places—my neck, my wrist and my chest. I was feeling like a survivor just like Beyonce for holding my head up after all I've been through. I blew myself a kiss in the mirror and headed out to the party.

I hopped on the subway dirty backpack style. I figured I needed to be obvious about having weed. Unfortunately, though, I couldn't hide my goodies. Niggas were staring at me left and right. But I thought if that was any indication, I would have them eating out of my hands in no time.

I arrived at the party and saw some of the same niggas I begged for work letting down their hair and being all nonchalant. I would never be so relaxed in the game. Neither was my dad. That's why he was so successful and climbed so high. He was a part of me and I planned to follow in his footsteps in a real serious way.

I decided to chill, sitting back and checking things out before I decided to make any moves.

Rodman was right about the scene. Heads were blazing weed all around me. Nobody gave a shit about the cops raiding the place. They were just getting their swerve on and trying to have a good time.

When I heard someone ask *Who has the smoke?* I decided it was time for me to make my move. I pulled out the blunt that I'd rolled earlier and told the nigga to try my shit out.

"If it's free, it's for me," he said before sparking it up with his lighter. "Goddamn, cutie! You're fine as hell and you got the bomb-ass dro. Can a nigga marry you or something?"

"I don't think so," I said with a laugh. "But there's more where that came from if you'd like to make a purchase."

"No doubt. I sure the fuck would," he said, handing me a fifty. "Let me get all of that. My ass will be flying through the clouds all week with this shit."

"Hold up," I said before dipping into a dark corner. I went into my backpack and pulled out five dime bags and a little extra from my private stash that I planned to test out later that evening. I wanted to thank him for buying so much.

"Here you go, my nig," I said when I got back to him.

He looked at what I handed him and smiled. I could tell he was pleased with the little extra something.

"Shorty, I think you're the woman of my dreams," he said. "Let me show you around to the people that be gettin' their blaze on. I can see you're about your paper."

"That's what's up," I said, happy that getting rid of the weed was gonna be easier with his help.

An hour later, I had less than two hundred dollars worth of weed left to sell. Niggas were buying the shit up then smoking it up like it was going out of style.

I thanked Sid Money, my first customer. He introduced me to just about everyone at the party.

"Come on, Tammy," Sid Money said. "I have a couple

more cats I want you to meet."

"You keep this up, nigga, and I'll be out of here before David Letterman comes on," I said jokingly.

"Awe, my damn, then I don't think I can help you no more," he said, teasing. "I want you to stay and party a little bit after you get rid of your product."

"I guess I can think about it," I replied and followed him as he walked up to a couple of Cuban dudes.

"What's up Carlo? Juan?" Sid Money said, shaking the hands of the two Cubans. "This is…"

"Tamika Jefferson," the guy named Carlo said.

I was surprised to say the least.

"Damn, man. How the fuck you know that?" Sid Money asked.

"You can't see the resemblance?" Carlo asked. "Look at those eyes. They can tear a whole in somebody's head when they're staring at ya. Then look at those cheekbones and lips."

"Man, what the hell are you talking about?" Sid Money asked.

"You're introducing me to royalty, my man," Carlo said. "This girl I already know. Well, I don't know her but I know of her. This is Marley's daughter, man. This is the big man's seed."

"Damn. You're fucking shittin' me!" Sid Money exclaimed. "Wait. Now that you mention it. I can see it.

Excuse the fuck out of me. I'm helping the big man's daughter pass off some weed."

"Weed? What the fuck do you mean weed?" Carlo asked.

I was starting to feel very exposed.

"She has that sticky, icky, man," Sid Money said jokingly, "She's got some hydro from another planet. She sold me some. That's why I'm swerving, man."

"You got that shit from Rodman, didn't you?" Carlo asked.

"I don't know what you're talking about," I said, knowing that you never give up your connection.

"Yeah. That's that nigga's shit," Carlo said. "He's been riding your dad's balls ever since I can remember. That nigga tryna get put down. But check this out. That nigga's too small time for a chick like you."

"Whatever," I said, acting a little interested but not too much. "I ain't see nobody else that's supposed to be a big boy tryna put me down."

"That's because we been waiting for you to get a clue or buy a vowel or something," Carlo said.

"I don't know what that's supposed to mean," I said, balling up my fists. I wasn't about to let a Cuban motherfucker try to play me out.

"Chill, chill, ma," Carlo said, laughing. "Didn't I tell y'all she's Marley's child. Look at her, ready to throw her hands up wit' the quickness."

"I don't think it's funny," I said, still irked.

"Ma, what I'm trying to say to you is that nobody that's a captain or lieutenant is gonna hire you to work for them when you're already the fucking General. Get a clue, ma. Get a clue."

"Sid Money, what the fuck is he talking about?" I asked.

"You don't know?" Sid Money asked. "You really don't fucking know?"

"Know what, nigga? Damn!" I snapped.

"Listen, ma," Carlo explained calmly. "Your dad left you a piece of his business that he wants you to run—a three hundred ninety million dollar piece to be exact. So you need to chill wit' your weed sells. They be having undercovers at these parties sometimes. That's how you can get hot. You would think that someone like Rodman would know that. I guess that's why your dad never put him on."

"Wait a minute. Back the fuck up to the three hundred ninety million dollar part," I said. I felt myself tingling all over like I just had an orgasm. "I ain't got time to be playing fucking games—especially about money that long."

"Well, ain't nobody playing games, ma. It's true," Carlo said. "Your dad has you set for life. You can run the business and flip that money he left you several times to become a billionaire, or you can sell it and walk away with all the straight cash right now. It's your choice."

"Well, I'll be goddamned," I said, rubbing my chin with

my hand. "My dad is the shit. He always looked out." I started laughing. "And I've been crawling on the floor begging for crumbs when all this time I could'a been chillin' at the head of the table." I looked up in the air. "I love you Dad, wherever you are. I fucking love you, man."

I started tearing. Sid Money attempted to console me. But when he put his arm around me, I jumped back.

"Careful, man," Carlo warned. "You know she's bodying niggas if they put their hands on her."

Everyone started to laugh. Sid Money looked like his hands got stuck in the cookie jar.

"Seriously, I ain't mean nothing by it," he said, a little shook and more than a little confused.

"It's cool," I said, grabbing Sid Money and placing his head on my shoulder. "This nigga's harmless. And to prove it…" I grabbed his face with both hands like the Italians do and kissed him flat on the lips. "Good looking, Sid Money. Thanks for all your help tonight."

I turned to walk away and heard everyone congratulating Sid Money. I strolled out of the party and headed home, trying to be cool even though I wanted to jump up and down and shout "I'm rich bitch!"

Life was finally looking up for me. I was on my way. Nothing was gonna stop me.

CHAPTER FIFTEEN

Tamika Meets Ramos

I heard banging on the door as I turned off the shower.

"Shit! That's all I fucking need," I said to myself as I quickly toweled off and slipped into my robe.

I ran to the door and yanked it open, irritated. Carlo's pearly whites are smiling at me.

"What the fuck are you doing here?" I asked.

"Don't you wanna get started running your business, ma?" Carlo asked.

"Yeah, I do. But how the fuck did you know where I live?" I asked.

"Ma, I took the liberty of tracking your ass last night after you left the party. Can't let royalty go around unprotected. Besides, the UOJB knows everything," he explained. "Everything."

I didn't know what he was talking about, but I didn't want

to get into a long, drawn out discussion about it either. At least not while I was standing there without any clothes on.

"Chill right here," I said. "Give me a minute."

I closed the door before Carlo had a chance to respond.

A few minutes later, I was in Carlo's car. It was a custom silver Cadillac Expedition. With cherrywood paneling, plush leather seats, a DVD player in back and an blazing sound system, it was the most luxurious car I'd ever been in.

"Can I ask you something, Carlo? If I'm the boss, why am I walking while you're riding around in this plush shit?"

"You're right, you are the boss, ma," he said. "But you ain't the boss of me. You have to learn a little more about the organization so you can start recognizing the levels and who's supposed to be treated like what. In the meantime, if you want a ride, buy yourself a ride."

"With what money?" I asked, looking at Carlo like he was a dunce.

"Ma, your credit's good with any establishment in New York and half the states on the east coast," Carlo responded. "It's not my fault you never tried to use it."

"True that," I said before leaning back and bobbing my head to the music, enjoying the ride.

Carlo parked the Caddy in front of a bunch of Cubans on Flatbush Avenue in Brooklyn.

"Tammy, I'd like for you to meet Ramos."

Ramos looked like he was the leader of the crew. He wasn't all that tall or all that built or all that handsome. He looked like the original Scarface. But the strength that emanated from him made him sexy as hell.

"Nice to meet you, Ramos," I said with flirty eyes.

I had woken up in a cold sweat that morning and took care of my needs in the shower. But for the first time in a long time, I realized that I hadn't had a dick in me for over six years. I did dream every now and then about how Cappy made me come with his mouth. It disgusted me to think about him. I hated the motherfucker. But I can't front. He gave me an orgasm like I never had.

Hah, I thought, *I should call myself the Black Widow. Fuck the shit out of them then kill them when I'm done.*

"Tammy, Tammy, hello…" Carlo said, snapping his fingers.

"Oh, my bad," I said. "I drift off from time to time thinking about my old demons."

"Well, I'm gonna have to help get you some new ones," Ramos said, holding out his hand. "It's a pleasure to meet you." I gave him my hand and he didn't hesitate to kiss it. "So. I've been holding a ton of money for you for years. Do you plan on cashing in or continuing what your father started?"

"I love tradition," I said. "So I'm definitely going to keep up with it. But I need a little something to hold me over. It's not good for me to be hanging around on the broke tip, being who I am and all."

"Well, it's only gonna cost two ninety to get your normal stock," Ramos said. "What the hell am I supposed to do with the other hundred million? It's not peanuts you know."

"Let me ask you a question. Is it exactly three ninety or is it three ninety and change?"

"It's three ninety-three," Ramos said. "But what's the point? That's still a lot of donuts to be trying to eat."

"It is for one person," I said. "But if you have a smorgasbord and invite a lot of people, they'll be able to help eat it all."

"Excuse me?" Ramos asked.

"I'm elated that my squad held things down for me while I was locked down," I said. "I hear I have a hundred people who report directly to me, right? And many others on the squads?"

"That's right," Ramos answered.

"Well, I want each of my hundred people to get a million. Sort of like a gesture of good will, you know, to let people know that there are no hard feelings and to reward them in advance for putting up with me. I'm gonna be real hard on niggas. But they can't keep it all to themselves. They have to share the money with their crews however they see fit but everybody's gotta eat and know it was from me. You, Carlo, and me get a million each of what's left over. Everybody will be fat and happy and ready to make money. All I want is insurance. I don't need the silver spoon. I want to start as close to scratch as possible. I want to earn their respect on my own."

"I hear that," Ramos agreed. "But Carlo, can she do this? I mean can she do it without speaking to Marley first?"

"Marley says it's her shit, man," Carlo answered. "She can do whatever the fuck she wants."

"Well, if it's cool with him, it's cool with me," Ramos said. "I just don't want no shit later when Marley hears about it."

"There won't be any shit," I told him. "I get what I want and this is how I want to start my business."

I turned back to Carlo's ride but I heard Ramos talking to Carlo.

"Please remind her that I don't work for her," Ramos said.

"You gotta do that yourself, man," Carlo replied. "I'm having enough trouble getting her to see that I don't work for her either."

I chuckled inside. *Not even a day has gone by since I learned that I was the queen and I'm already trying to run things my way. I guess I am my father's child.*

CHAPTER SIXTEEN

School's in Session

I woke up all turned on again. There was something to not having to worry about where my next meal was coming from that made me feel horny as hell. And then there was Ramos. I didn't dream about Cappy's sorry-ass. My mind drifted to Ramos and his strong hands. I wondered how they would feel on my silky smooth skin as he explored my body.

After my shower, I padded into the kitchen and attempted to make myself a cup of coffee with the fancy coffee machine I bought after my meeting with Carlo and Ramos.

If you're gonna be privileged, you have to act privileged, I told myself.

I read the instructions and pressed START. It worked! I brewed myself a cup of cappuccino. It was delicious.

I was about to turn on the television and kick my feet up on the coffee table when I heard a knock on the door.

"Shit," I said as I stomped over to the door. "I didn't even get a chance to turn the damned TV on!"

"You sleep rather late for someone who's supposed to be the boss," Ramos quipped when I opened the door.

I was embarrassed. He caught me in my pajamas.

"Don't any of you guys know how to call before coming over?"

"Oh, is this for me?" Ramos grabbed my cup of cappuccino, sat down and took a sip.

I was annoyed. I hadn't offered him a seat and he knew damned well I didn't offer him my coffee.

"Umm, excuse me," I said, snatching my coffee mug out of his hand.

"Watch it! You could have burned me!"

"And that'd be what you deserve for touching shit that don't belong to you," I snapped.

"And you don't have time to be sipping coffee," he snapped right back. "We have a lot of shit to do today and you're sleeping in like you're a nightclub promoter or something. Haven't you ever heard about the early bird catching the worm."

"I may have heard that in another life," I said, before taking a sip of my coffee. "Now what's up?" I asked.

"Not you, ma," Ramos said. "I'm not joking. I need you to get a move on. We have lots of shit to do today and you have a shitload of people to meet."

I didn't say a word. I grabbed my coffee mug and dragged myself to my bedroom.

I can't be mad at Ramos. I'm sure my dad didn't make it big by being as lax as I've been the past couple of days. He probably put in a lot of hard work. Right now I'm acting like a spoiled bitch with a silver spoon in her mouth—the exact shit I said I wouldn't do.

I brushed my teeth, washed my face, and threw on some sweat shorts and a pair of Coach sneakers. I planned to be low key when I met everyone. I didn't need anybody drooling at me.

When I was happy with my appearance, I headed downstairs, still carrying the little bit of coffee I had left.

"Let's get something straight, Ramos," I said when I got downstairs. "I'm a dragon in the morning so don't fuck with me before I've had my coffee."

"I guess that means I should never drink your coffee either?" Ramos asked, smiling.

"You're a fast learner," I said. "Let's bounce."

We rode throughout the five boroughs of New York City, making five and ten minute stops here and there.

Brooklyn, the Bronx, Harlem, and Long Island were sewn up. Not much was happening in Manhattan except for Gramercy and the Village. I made a mental note to move into Manhattan by working things out with the Italians.

All the while, Ramos told me about my newly inherited cocaine and heroin businesses which spanned from Latin America—the part under Ramos' control—to Haiti, then to Venezuela, and finally to New York.

He also explained how our New York portion of the channel was strong because of the Unity of Jamaican Brother, a fraternity of hard-nosed criminals that wouldn't let anything come between it and its members.

"Many Latin Americans won't even fuck with you if you aren't a part of the UOJB," Ramos said. "They figure if the UOJB doesn't trust you, then they shouldn't trust you."

"I guess I'm gonna have to be in the UOJB, then," I said.

"You will, in time," Ramos promised. "But don't rush it. You may not be ready yet for some of the requirements."

"Like what?" I ask.

"Forget it, for now, Mamita," he said. "We have a lot of other shit to work on."

"I ain't scared of shit, Ramos," I said.

"No one is saying that you are but maybe you should be," he said. "Sometimes fear is a better motivator than anything else. It feeds your adrenaline and gets your heart pumping enough to do anything. Sometimes fear can save your life."

I knew he was right but I didn't want to seem like a punk.

"Well, the thrill of battle gets my heart pumping," I said. "Looking someone in the eyes that just fucked up and fucked with the wrong person is all the adrenaline I need to do just about anything. I will not be punked by anyone."

"I guess this is a subject we're not gonna get anywhere with," Ramos said. "So since you already got a body, Cappy I'm talking about, you have to kill one or two more people before UOJB would even consider letting you in. All UOJB members have at least two or three bodies on their resumé."

"That's good to know," I said. "At least I won't be consorting with punks."

Ramos gave me a look that said, "Calm the fuck down."

But I didn't plan to. I was so ready to take the game by storm, making a mark that my dad would be proud of. I just needed to finish finding out about the Who, What, When, Where and Why's?

CHAPTER SEVENTEEN

Graduation

It took about a week to meet and greet all of my captains, lieutenants, and even quite a few street soldiers.

I met lookout boys, chefs, gun connections, and some of the members of the UOJB. I was pretty much set. All I had to do was seal the deal whenever I was ready.

Truth be told, I couldn't have been any more ready. It was like I had stepped outside myself and was playing the lead in a gangster movie. I was ready to shoot up the entire town if I had to. Whatever it took to get my respect.

I decided to rob a bank in midtown Manhattan. It didn't get any more gully than that.

I rolled up on the bank and double parked until a spacious spot opened up in front. I parked the car, feeling glad that I'd be able to do what I had to do after the robbery went down.

I reached into the bag in the passenger seat and grabbed my President Richard Nixon mask. Then I glanced out at the meter to make sure I had a few minutes to do what I was going to do. I did.

This won't take long, I thought. *Ain't no use in feeding the meter when I'll be in and out in no time.*

I bent down, put on my mask and grabbed my AK-47 from under the passenger seat. Then I took a deep breath before getting out of the car.

I rushed into the bank, knocking over some old lady.

"Alright, this is a hold-up!" I screamed, blasting a few rounds in the ceiling. "No one will get hurt if no one tries to get cute."

The security guard apparently didn't hear me because he went for his gun.

Bitt, bitt, bitt, bitt, pow!!

I let off a few rounds that put the would-be hero out of his misery.

"Again, everyone on the floor!" I screamed. "Don't try to be fucking heroes! Fill up this bag with small bills." I threw a small satchel over the counter at one of the tellers.

She moved robotically, shaking as she followed my orders. Before long, the bag was filled to the top with an assortment of fives, tens, twenties and fifties.

I grabbed the satchel heavy with money and backed

towards the bank door. Another asshole made a move. I blasted his ass just as I did the first dude.

The other security guard looked me in my eye like he was scared. But he also looked pissed.

Bitt, bitt, bitt, bitt, pow!!

I blasted his ass, too, then ran out the door.

I jumped in the car and peeled off, heading for the other car I stashed.

I reached the car in no time and the switch went off without a hitch. I reduced my speed, drove a couple of blocks and coasted over to the UOJB meeting place.

When I walked into the restaurant, everyone was watching the Breaking News bulletin on TV. I watched footage of myself in the President Nixon mask busting off in the bank then jumping in my getaway car. Everyone was in awe, saying how ruthless I was. And they had no idea it was me. That made me smile.

I cleared my throat real loud to let everyone know the queen had arrived. Then very dramatically, I flicked the President Nixon mask and the satchel of money onto the floor.

Fifty stunned faces looked back at me. Ramos recovered the quickest.

"Well, well. Here's the woman of the hour right now!" Ramos exclaimed.

I could tell he was impressed with me. Hell, everybody was. I could see the respect in their eyes as Ramos began to introduce me around the room. All except for this one cat named Prago. I couldn't stand the way he was gritting on me. I kept cool, though. I was the newcomer and there was no reason to start shit with someone who was obviously drunk out of his head.

"Did you see how she blasted those motherfuckers?" Ramos asked. "I told you she had it in her."

There were cheers and drinks all around. Everyone was patting me like I was a hero. Everyone except for Prago.

It went on like that for about fifteen minutes until Prago had had enough.

"Goddamn, men!" he said, "It was a fucking off-duty cop and two security guards. What the fuck should we give her? A cookie?"

Bang. Bang.

I smoked his ass with my forty-five.

"I can't stand a hatin'-ass nigga," I snapped.

"Mamita, what have you done?" Ramos asked, unbelieving. "Prago was talking shit 'cuz he was drunk. He's always doing that shit."

"Well not anymore," I said.

And then I was in. I was a member of UOJB. There was nothing left to stand in my way.

By the time we left the restaurant, I was so drunk, I could hardly stand up. Ramos wasn't doing that much better but he managed to drive me home.

He helped me out of his truck and walked me to my door. I leaned heavily on his shoulder and he placed an arm around my waist to steady me. I couldn't tell if he was being fresh or if he was really just trying to hold both of us up.

I fumbled with the key several times before I got it in the lock. Ramos and I were leaning on the door and practically fell down when I finally got it open. We made it to the couch and crashed. I was glad we made it to something soft.

I struggled to a sitting position and grabbed Ramos's hand. We half carried each other to the stairs, laughing the whole way, and then struggled up the stairs. When we made it to the bed, Ramos fell first and I fell on top of him.

The feeling of his body under mine sobered me up. It had been so long since I had any. The situation was not good. But it was too late.

My hormones were raging and I needed something to take the edge off.

"Mamita? Can you get off me?" Ramos asked.

"Can you make me?" I shot back. "Hmm. Can you make me?" I giggled and poked him in his side.

"If you keep doing that, you're gonna make me throw up, Mamita."

"Sorry. But I'm still not getting up until you make me."

"So, you want me to make you, Mamita?" he asked. "Huh, do you want me to make you?"

He was as drunk as I was and his words came out slurred but I knew what he meant.

He started to wrestle with me but he was rubbery. He couldn't budge me. We went back and forth but it was no use.

I grabbed his arms and locked them back over his head. "Do you give up?" I asked.

"You are such a control freak," he said but I saw that his eyes were clearing a little. He seemed surprised by my aggression.

"So," I said.

"Do you have to control every situation?" he asked me.

"I'm a big girl. I'm supposed to be in control."

"Is that right?" he asked with a smile curling on his lips.

"It's more than right. It's the law."

I bent down and kissed him hungrily on his sexy lips. He graciously accepted my kiss.

Before long, we were rolling around naked, practicing on making a baby.

When he tenses up and shot his fluid inside of me, I thought, *Finally something has put out the fire burning inside of me. Now I can concentrate on getting some work done.*

CHAPTER EIGHTEEN

The Executioner

I spent the better part of the following month on my One a Day Program. But I wasn't taking any pills. It seemed that I was busting a nigga's ass at least once a day.

Ramos thought I was wilding out but I wasn't. I always had a good reason.

For instance, one soldier called me a bitch so I bitch slapped him with the butt of my forty-five then turned it around to body his ass. Then there was the guy who talked back at me when I was reprimanding him for dishing out credit.

"There is no fucking credit, dumb-ass," I snapped.

Boww. Boww. Boww.

I bodied his ass, too.

In total, I killed twenty-eight people, twenty-six of whom were on my team. I did what I had to do to build discipline and maintain order. And I built a team that respected me and would never question me.

Ramos arrived at my house one day with a funny look on his face, the same look he wore when he bodied several other crew members, so I knew where he was about to go.

"Look, Ramos, the shit would'a never happened if…"

"If what, Mamita?" he asked me. "If what? You can't keep killing off your crew. Sooner or later, you won't have any crew. Don't you know these people have families? You're creating beef where there is none."

"Look, I have to do what I have to do," I said. "You don't know how it is to be taken lightly just because you have tits instead of balls. I work my ass off for respect. So what should I do when a nigga disrespects me?"

"Tamika, he spilled his fucking beer," Ramos snapped, sounding frustrated.

"Is that how the story got back to you?" I asked. He raised his eyebrows as if I was going to feed him some bullshit. "Ramos, for real, what had happened was…"

"Wait. Let me sit down," he said. "This is going to be a good, I'm sure."

"For real, though, Ramos." I could barely contain my laughter. "We were all standing there, chillin'. The sets were flowing so a few lieutenants and a couple of captains were hanging out with me having a beer in an alleyway. This soldier comes up. You know the one, Petey. Anyway, he asks for a beer and one of the lieutenants says, 'Think fast,' and throws him one. The nigga had it in his hands then dropped it. The shit got all over my Prada boots. I know that nigga did the shit on purpose so I blasted his ass. That's the same nigga that was mad before, giving his lieutenant lip about one of the directives I laid down. He wanted payback but look who really got paid back. His ass is six feet fucking deep."

"He may be six feet deep, Tammy, but you're deep," Ramos said.

"What? No more, Mamita?" I asked.

"Today's not a Mamita kind of day," he said. "You're wildin' out. Anyway, I have some good news and some bad news."

"Oh shit. Give me the fucking bad news first. Maybe the good news will make the bad news sting less."

"Well, the bad news is that your old man is not happy with your behavior," Ramos informed me.

"He's all the way in Jamaica, though. By the time he gets the stories they have been changed around and around. He really should just kick it with me to find out the real shit."

"I guess that's his intention and part of the good news. You know Marley doesn't trust phones. He wants to hear what's going on straight from the horse's mouth," Ramos paused. "You're going to Kingston."

"Oh shit! For real? I get to see Dad? Ain't no bad news

about that, Ramos! You had me sweatin' around the collar for nothing. Damn! After all these years, I get to hug my dad."

I was so choked up, Ramos put his arms around me. I hugged him back tightly. It felt good.

"Let me find out you're catching feelings," I said through my sniffles.

"What? You're doing the crying, Mamita," he said. "What am I supposed to do, ignore you?"

"As long as you know that we're friends," I said. "Kinda like fuck buddies. I like your sex and think you like mine but no one needs to be getting caught up. It's too dangerous given the life we are both living."

"I feel you, ma," he agreed. "But I still think this is a good time to celebrate."

"Is that so?" I asked.

He nodded his head and planted a wet kiss on my mouth. I put my hands on his shoulders and started pushing him down to his knees.

Wasting no time, I loosened the cord on my sweat pants and pushed them and my thong down.

Ramos didn't waste any time either. He palmed my ass cheeks then dove head first—no tongue first—into my clean-shaven pussy. He licked me like a dog dying of thirst, trying to lap up every hint of moisture emanating from my body. The sensation sent chills up my spine.

I felt myself getting close but I wanted him to stop. I didn't want to come that way. I want it all. I wanted to feel him inside of me.

I pulled myself away and turned around. Then I grabbed his hand and guided him up off his knees. Once he stood up, I started stroking his dick through his pants.

He feverishly pulled off his pants and boxers. His dick sprung out and stood at attention, ready for action as always. He adjusted himself behind me and put his shaft into my wet, pleading love box.

He stroked me slowly but I wanted it faster. I started throwing myself back onto his dick.

"Faster!" I hissed. "Get this pussy, Ramos. Get this pussy. Smack my ass like I like."

He obliged me and started giving it to me just like I like—rough, rugged and raw.

In ten minutes, his intense grinding came to a stop as he came inside me. My wetness eagerly accepted his. The experience made me feel rejuvenated.

"So, what time are you coming over?" I asked when I felt like we'd both calmed down enough.

"I still can't stay the night?" he asked.

"Ramos, what did I say earlier about catching feelings?" I asked matter-of-factly.

"We've fucked every night for a month, Mamita. And after we finish you always kick me out. You haven't let me stay once."

"Listen, Ramos, I like you," I said. "In fact, I have serious love for you. You've been a big help in my business life and a good friend in my personal life. But why are you running a marathon. Just relax and take things slow. You said it yourself. You're getting the best piece of pussy that New York City has to offer—and every night. Do you wanna fuck that up by going against the grain? Do you?"

"I guess I don't, ma," he said. But I could tell he was pissed. "I guess I better be going. I'll be here at five-thirty to take you to LaGuardia."

"Don't be mad at me, Ramos."

"I'm fine," he said.

"No you're not."

"Really, I'm fine," he lied again.

"So why are you rushing off without giving me a kiss?"

He turned around at the door, grabbed me and pushed his tongue into my mouth. I loved kissing Ramos. It was always so erotic and sexy.

"I knew you weren't decent so I didn't want you to be near the door when I left." He continued to lie, trying to save face.

"Ramos, I don't give a shit who knows that we're fucking," I snapped. "I'll shout it out the door if you'd like. All of New York can see you leaving here palming my naked ass. As long as you understand that we need to calm down and take things slow. Comprendes?

"Si. Comprendo."

I leaned against the door frame and wrapped my arms around my body tightly. Too bad I had to hide my real feelings. Women had gotten the short end of the stick in love for far too long and I wasn't going to let it happen to me.

Well, at least he tapped that ass right before he left.

CHAPTER NINETEEN

Tamika Travels to Kingston

The wheels of the plane touched down on the runway in Kingston and I felt as excited as a ten-year-old child.

I saw a group of Jeeps up ahead as the plane taxied to a stop. I was getting more and more excited, wondering if my dad was amongst the welcoming party.

Regrettably, when my escort, Caesar, led me to the vehicles, I saw that my dad wasn't there. The men who were sent to pick me up were part of my dad's security force. They were all ready to give their lives to ensure safety. They made sure that my plane wasn't intercepted or hijacked.

"OK, Rude-gal. We go. There is much about Jamaica that you need to learn."

For the better part of three hours, Caesar drove me around Kingston, pointing things out here and there. If I had a dollar for every time he started a sentence with "Rude-gal" I would have added another million to my pocket.

"Rude-gal, do you see how da goats have more mind in their heads than the people? The goats walk along the pavement safely while the jigglers dodge the crissers in the street."

"What's a jiggler, Caesar?" I asked. "And what's a crisser?"

"Rude-gal, a jiggler is a street vendor. They always tell you high price since they know you gon' fight with them over the fee. It's how they bargain with you. Don't ever accept the first offer. Now a crisser, that's just a late model car. I believe that in America you call them hoopties."

"Yeah, I've seen quite a few hoopties in my day," I said, laughing. "Luckily, I don't have to drive in no bullshit like that, though."

"Respect, you are royalty, Rude-gal," Caesar swooned. "There isn't a crisser in the world made for you. But speaking of cars, will you be needing one while you are here?"

"No, Caesar, I won't. I'm just gonna take taxis, I guess. I don't want to get lost."

"Kingston is a very dangerous place," he said. "Rude-boys, gangs and shottas are everywhere. You cannot get lost around here. I will see to it by taxiing you around myself. But if I have something to do and can't drive you, remember this. Always agree on a price with a driver before he drives away.

He will double charge you as fast as he would rob you blind."

"I'm not worried about that, Caesar," I said. "I can handle myself."

"That you can, Rude-gal. That you can."

"Rude-gal, Rude-gal, look there..." he pointed past a bridge. "That is the Torrington Bridge. You never want to go past there by yourself. That's where you'll find the ghettoes of Southside, Rema, Jungle, and Lizard Town. People never stray too far away from home there, especially at night."

"Jungle, that sounds interesting," I said. "I think I want to go there."

"It is full of Rude-boys and gangs," Caesar warned. "You do not have to go there. You are royalty. You have soldiers to journey those parts for you."

"There's nothing I won't ask a soldier to do that I wouldn't do myself," I said. "I lead by example, not by fear. I'll look a snake in the eyes and bite its head off if I had to."

Caesar cringed but didn't say anything. I was certain that he didn't want to travel in the Jungle.

Caesar pointed out buildings that used to be prominent in their day.

"These places were thriving once... no more," he said sadly. "They were neglected and forgotten just like our people. The corrupt government turned our paradise into

Babylon, full of duty shotta police boys, armies, devil politicians, and scum businessmen—all stealing from the people. There were three murders a day around here not long ago. Because our people are starving, they join the fight."

I shook my head as he pointed at a woman pushing a stroller.

"No doubt she push a killed baby with no insides," he said, clearly irritated. "They clean out the guts then repackage them with the dust of death. Then she mule push the girl like she were asleep. And she probably swallowed a condom herself..."

"Why would she swallow a condom?" I interrupted, feeling nauseated.

"Them stuff the condoms with cocaine tablets then them mule girls swallow them. Scotland Yard says that one out of three Jamaican nationals on a plane are drug mules. Yeah, mon. We beat the system. No locks or keys or security screens at tight borders can stop us from winning out over our Babylon oppressors. Oh shit," he snapped nervously. "Here goes one now."

He slowed the car down to a reasonable speed. He had been driving well above the limit all along.

"Careful now," he whispered. "Him was trained by Colonel Trevor MacMillan himself."

"Who's Colonel MacMillan?" I asked.

"He was a JDF, a Jamaican Defense Force officer and ex

Commissioner of Police. But this guy over there is named Baobi. He's as ruthless and corrupt as they come. He gives your dad many problems. He gives everyone problems. Tis why I be careful. I don' want him to see me and extort me."

"So he gives us problems, huh?" I asked. A wicked smile appeared on my face. "We should follow him then."

"Follow him? We wan' stay far, far away from Baobi," he said cautiously.

"No. We want to follow him," I said. "Trust me. It's for the best."

We followed Baobi out of the bad neighborhoods and kept our distance as the landscape started to improve. All was going well until Caesar started to act nervous again.

"What's wrong, Caesar?" I asked.

"He is approaching Up Park Camp," he said. "That must be where he's going. Up Park Camp is the home of the JDF. It is not safe for people like us."

"Don't worry, Caesar. I got this," I said. Nervously and reluctantly, he continued to follow Baobi.

"OK, Caesar. Pull up next to him," I ordered.

"What?"

"Pull up next to him," I ordered again.

Caesar followed my instructions and pulled up next to Baobi. Baobi was a petite, extremely dark, thin man with devilish red eyes and a sinister looking mouth.

BOWW. BOWW. BOWW. I clicked off three rounds.

Baobi's car careened into a building and exploded. Caesar slowed and made a U turn. I made sure he didn't speed as we drove away.

"You are truly a Rude-gal," Caesar said. "Many a Rude-boy would be feared to do what you did. Don't worry, though. Kingston is so cruel right now that Rude-boys and gangs, them cocky as they come. They threaten you on the street in plain view then kill you without an eye blink. They kill duty shotta police boys in uniform or in them house clothes. Them no care. JDF know that them no care. But Baobi, that's too much. JDF will swear him was assassinated."

I could tell that Caesar was shaken up by my gangster. But fuck it. I was not gonna have people messing with my dad just like he wouldn't have people messing with me.

CHAPTER TWENTY

Tamika in the UK

Caesar took me to the Jungle after we left Up Park Camp. I was feeling extremely relaxed after breaking my cherry in Kingston.

We went to an area where we've had problems. I felt like Miss Fix-It so that's what I planned to do.

"This is it, Rude-gal," Caesar said. "This is the area."

I looked around and saw shanties, shacks and broken down wooden huts. An abomination of a so-called neighborhood.

"So are you sure you want to be here?" he asked.

"Sometimes, you gotta do what you gotta do," I said. "Just point out the posse when we get to it."

As we crept along, I heard people whispering on the street. They were wondering who I was, wondering why I was letting them see my AK-47. But I think they knew because I heard my father's named whispered several times.

I wanted to see my dad but I knew I had a few things to do before. After all that Caesar had told me, I felt responsible to take care of a few problems for my dad.

As Caesar pointed out a crew of Rude-boys ahead, his cell phone rang. He answered it but kept driving slowly just as I had earlier instructed him.

"Yes... me soon come," Caesar said. "Soon. We soon come."

As he was wrapping up his conversation, I hopped out of the Jeep and blasted the air. I dusted off every member of the crew that was giving us problems. Then I hopped back in the Jeep.

"Let's go," I said.

"No. We be safe, man. We soon come. OK. We soon come. Bye."

Caesar closed the phone. "Rude-gal, Marley gon' think I put his kin in danger. Now we have to get rid of this car and get another one. You gon' get me killed."

"No. Things are fine," I said. "Dad knows how I am. You were only doing as you were told. Just get us where we need to go and let me handle my dad."

A little while later we were back in the good part of town. Caesar and I switched Jeeps and made our way to my dad's mansion.

"My job is done, Miss Jefferson," Caesar said. "Go up the walkway and ring the bell. One of the attendants will take your bags. Enjoy your stay in Kingston."

"Thanks," I said as Caesar sped off. Then I slowly took the walkway to the gatehouse.

The adrenaline from the kills had worn off and what replaced it was an excitement I hadn't felt in years. I was going to see my daddy again!

"My baby!" Dad exclaimed. I hadn't even rung the bell. "How was your flight? How are you?"

He had scooped me up into his arms and was swinging me around like he did when I was a little girl. Tears of joy covered both our faces.

Dad peppered me with a million questions.

"Dad, I'd answer you if I could! But you're holding me so tight I hardly breathe!"

"Sorry, baby," he said. "But look at you. Look at you! You're all grown up and you're gorgeous! Tamika, you could be a supermodel or something! But instead you become a vigilante? Do you know how disappointed I am in you? I love you to pieces and it's amazing to see you. But I am so disappointed in you."

"Dad, you're talking too fast. I've missed you so much. But you have no idea what I've been through."

"I can only imagine, Princess," he said sadly. "I can only imagine."

Dad took me to his library, a huge bright room that over-looked rugged cliffs that dropped down to the sparkling blue sea, and made me comfortable on a plush white sofa. He had a servant bring us fresh fruit and cool drinks and then started asking his questions again.

We talked for hours about everything—Mom, Cappy, the business, my life, his life, my prison stay, his prison stay—we totally caught up with each other's lives over the past dozen years.

At the end of our talk, I learned that I would be leaving for the UK the next day. Dad said he'd be joining me but wouldn't stay as long as he had arranged for me to stay.

"See, Tamika," he said. "You have been trying to move too fast. Sometimes in life you need to just chill. Unfortunately for you, it's too late for that. That's why the UOJB in the UK asked me to recruit you to help them sort out a few of their problems. Seems your reputation for being cold-blooded precedes you. And to make matters worse, you may end up at the helm by the time you go back to New York."

"Why do you seem so sad about it?" I asked. "I'm moving up in the world."

"Tamika, you don't get it," he said. "Petty jealousy and envy run rampant in this game. You think people love you because you're the new Ms. But people have been busting their asses for years to have what you have, to be where you are, and you're about to step over a lot of them. In their minds, they believe that I've handed everything to you on a silver platter."

I gave him a look that said I've put in my time—short time or not.

"It doesn't matter that you've done the work. It doesn't matter that you've been hustling while a lot of other people have been partying it up, acting sloppy. This game we play is very dangerous and we have to watch our backs at all times. There are a lot hatin'-ass niggas out there. And because you didn't take things slow, you've created plenty more of them. I hope you're happy."

Dad looked sad as hell as he walked away, like he just handed me a death sentence. He had given me the choice to take the money and run or run the business. I made my choice and I think he was kicking himself for not forcing me to take the money and run. But I told myself that I would be OK. I was a big girl and I could take care of myself. After all, I was the baddest bitch on the block.

We touched down at Heathrow Airport the next morning.

Roy, the Godfather and mentor of the UOJB in the UK, was going to meet me but I had no idea what he looked like. It didn't take me long, though, to figure it out.

Suddenly, one nigga pushed another and started running from him like he was running for his life. The other nigga was yelling at him to stop.

I stepped to the side as the runner neared me and I planted a right cross square on his jaw just as he was passing by. He fell to the ground. Roy's assistants came, scooped him up and disappeared.

"I knew I was not wrong about you, Ms. Tammy," Roy said as he escorted me to his vehicle. "We haven't officially met but already your presence is felt. You've just saved the UOJB many problems."

It turned out that the running man was named Alexander. He was a high ranking member in the UOJB who didn't want to take responsibility for one of his fuck-ups. He wanted one of his lower level soldiers to take the wrap.

The problem was that when the London police smelled blood, they didn't quit. It was not like in the US where someone can walk by snitching and making shady deals. If you fuck up in the UK, you do the time. Everyone in the British UOJB knew that. Roy assumed that Alexander was planning to make trouble for all its members.

"Many members have an if-I-go-down-you-go-down-with-me mentality," Roy explained. "And that is not good for business. It is never good for our business. So, we're straightening out the Alexander situation. We need you to deal with his people to make sure there are no more cancerous cells within our body. If there are, they must be destroyed. The UOJB must remain intact and healthy. As your reward, if you are successful, you will run the UOJB in New York City. All of this has been preordained. I hope that you're willing to be UOJB for life. Once sworn in, you can never leave voluntarily. We all go out like gangsters…"

"Or we don't go out at all," I said, finishing the motto.

"I'm glad we're on the same page, Ms. Tammy," Roy said. "Well, I won't detain you any longer. Here we are at UOJB headquarters. You have business to attend to."

CHAPTER TWENTY-ONE

Tamika Returns to Harlem and Meets Mom

I had never seen such loyalty as I experienced in the crime syndicate.

I smoked thirteen motherfuckers before leaving the UK. Alexander's crew had been properly handled and I felt good about it. And I wasn't worried one bit about Roy. My secrets were as safe with him as his were with me.

The world of professional organized crime was so much different from the petty nickel and dime shit I saw with the unorganized drug boys in Harlem when I was growing up. What I was involved in was something special.

Still, I was concerned about what Dad was concerned about. He wouldn't have brought it up if it wasn't an issue. I would never be sure where the next Benedict Arnold or Judas would come from. Who could I trust? Or better, could I trust anybody?

I was so jet-lagged when I got off the plane that when I saw my mom waiting for me at the gate, I thought I was hallucinating. But I wasn't.

"What are you doing here?" I asked her.

"Since you haven't been to see me, I figured I'd have to come calling for you."

"I've been busy," I said. I didn't have it in me to call her Mom.

"You should never be too busy for your family, Tamika," she said.

I gave her a look that could kill. Family? Was she kidding?

"I can't believe that you don't care that I'm penniless," she continued. "You haven't even checked on me. And it's not like you don't have any money. Look at you, Donna Karan." She reached out to touch my blouse. I pulled away. "It's not even the cheaper DKNY line. It's pure couture. I've always been there for you, Tamika. I don't deserve this."

"You've been there for me?" I said sarcastically. "Are you kidding? You told me that it was time for me to grow up when that nigga raped me. You told me to do my part and be nice whenever that asshole wanted to fuck me."

"I'm still your mother, Tamika."

"That's right. You are my mother," I said. "You're the same shitty-ass mother who let some nigga fuck your daughter. And all that time I repressed it, not wanting to look at you in a bad light. I wanted to be your daughter, to understand. How else was I supposed to look at you? I was a child. You were my mother. You were supposed to protect me. But all you cared about was yourself. You gambled on the wrong team and now you're paying for it. And I want you to know that I will never forgive you for what you did..."

"You won't forgive me?" she asked angrily. "I'm trying to find a way to forgive you."

"Forgive me?" I ask, stunned.

"You took my life away!" she screamed. "You took away all the hope I had."

"You know what? Mom. I don't have time for this," I said. "I'm very busy and you are slowing me down. I could be doing lots of things more important than this."

"What could be more important than talking to your mother today when I'm sure you know I have to turn myself in tomorrow to be deported?" she asked.

"I have a manicure and facial appointment," I said as sarcastically and vindictively as I could. "Good luck with that thing tomorrow."

I walked away, ignoring her call for me to go back. I have to admit it was painful. But I told myself that I had buried that part of my life that included her a long time ago. I didn't have time to revisit those particular demons. I had to be on point. Like Dad said, I didn't know what was going to happen when news of my promotion hit the streets. The last thing

I needed was to be thinking about my mom and her bullshit.

I asked Ramos to help me gather everyone at the social club. But I didn't tell him what was going down. I wanted everyone to hear it from Roy himself on a conference call.

The mood was festive and I had hoped that everything would go well once the news of my promotion got out. I didn't want things to get weird. Yet, I really didn't give a fuck. I deserved the promotion. I had done more work in the last year than most had done in a decade. And I was never one to rest on my laurels. UOJB's New York City contingent was about to get some real serious discipline.

I got chills when the phone rang. I felt nervous as hell. Still, I knew I couldn't turn back the hands of time and avoid the inevitable. Roy told me in no uncertain terms that the bigwigs wanted me. I just hoped that I was up to the task.

"Gentlemen, brothers," Roy's voice rang out from the speakers the phone was jacked into. "I hope all is well and I hope everyone is being careful." The group chimed in telling Roy that they were. "Good. I'm certain that you are. We insist that you take precautions to protect our security at all times. Now Miss Tammy, she's always careful. You can learn much from her. That's why we want all of you to follow her lead and direction. It's high time we've a leader like her in New York. I'm certain that everyone will support her. Good day, gentlemen."

Just like that he was gone, and all we heard from the speakerphone was the gentle hiss of the dial tone.

I had hoped Roy would say more. I stumbled to find the words to finish his report, hoping I wouldn't mess up.

"I was just as surprised as all of you when I was informed," I said. "But the law has been laid down and I'm not one to go against the grain. I'm gonna take a few days to figure out how I'm gonna do things but I don't see a lot changing. We have a pretty tight clique here and everyone seems to be pulling their weight," I lie. I have several slackers in mind. "Just keep handling your business. Don't let me stop you. I need some time to get myself together anyway."

I wanted to leave right then but I was slowed up by congratulatory hugs and kisses from the guys. Some of them were sincere but others weren't. Some hugged me mostly because it was their one and only chance to do so. I didn't care. I was just glad it was over so I could get back to being paranoid.

I was glad I didn't have to make any special gestures for Ramos to join me outside. He left when I did.

The niggas weren't stupid, though. They knew we were fucking. No matter hard we tried, it was impossible to hide our chemistry.

With all I had been dealing with and the stress that I just

inherited, I needed Ramos to tune me up in a serious way. I planned to fuck the shit out of him that night. And I decided I might even let him spend the night.

CHAPTER TWENTY-TWO

Tamika and Ramos in Trouble

I woke up with the walls of my pussy throbbing. Ramos wasn't really able to hang up in my tight coochie for that long without busting, but he held his own during rounds two and three. I should have told him to hit tar after he got his shit off the first time, though. But I was being selfish.

I went into the bathroom to take a quick shower and of course the soap stung when I washed my private parts.

I couldn't remember the last time I got it so good.

After cleaning off our fuck juices, I went into the bedroom and threw on a pair of sweat shorts. I felt totally refreshed and invigorated. There was nothing like a good piece of dick when it feels like the world is closing in on you.

I looked over at Ramos who was sleeping peacefully. For a split second, he looked like the devil to me but I immediately wiped that thought from my mind. Ramos would never turn on me. But since I was still in a constant state of paranoia, he had to get out of my bed.

I shook him and called his name repeatedly until he stirred.

"Ramos. Ramos! Come on, man. Get that ass up! Come on, Ramos! Shit."

"What's up, Mamita?" he asked when he finally rolled over.

"Not you, Ramos, and that's a problem. I let you sleep here last night and I'm not feeling good about it. So can you do me a favor?"

"I know, you want me to leave," he pouted.

"Come on, baby. Don't pout," I said. "I let you stay all night. That's a start for me."

"Say no more," he said. "I don't want to ruffle your feathers. I'm just thankful for last night."

I felt like he finally understood me. He left without incident.

Maybe things with him will work out, I thought.

I rode around the next few days taking mental notes of everything that was going on at our sets. Most things were on point but there was some sloppy shit that I planned to address. I wanted to wait until Friday, though. The fellas normally went to the club on Fridays anyway so I wouldn't have to call a special meeting. I'd catch them in their element. Maybe I'd even hear some of their boy talk before they knew that I as there.

I heard the fellas laughing up a storm when I parked my ride. Carlo's voice was ringing out above all of them. I wasn't sure what the fuck he was talking about but it seemed he had everyone rolling on the floor.

"Yeah, fellas," Carlo said, laughing—barely able to get it out. "Ramos says he fucks her silly. And the militant bitch is a freak at that. She even let my man cum on her face just like in the pornos."

In a word, I was livid. Livid, livid, livid.

I wasn't as mad at Carlo as I could have been. Men are always gonna talk shit. I was angry that Ramos was putting our business out on the street. And I was mad at myself for letting it happen. I knew better than to mix business with pleasure. Shit.

The night Carlo was talking about, I was drunk as hell. I was sucking Ramos's dick for the one and only time ever and it was getting good for him. I was so drunk, my reflexes were slow as hell. I pulled his dick out of my mouth before he came but I couldn't move away fast enough. Some of his cum got on my cheek. It grossed me out but I didn't trip that much because I was drunk, too. I also didn't trip because Ramos was so sweet, sensitive and understanding. Who'd a thought the motherfucker was playing me?

"Can you boys stop talking about my sex life long enough to have a quick meeting?" I asked.

They all looked at me like they were about to shit themselves, even Carlo who turned around like he just got caught murdering the President of the United States.

"We have some problems," I said. "Not with this. We have some problems on our sets."

I spelled everything out without mentioning what they were laughing about. Having a stiff upper lip was one of the things you needed if you were a woman in that business. You couldn't get all teary and shit and then command respect.

I handled my business and left. Moments after I got home, Ramos was knocking at my door.

"Mamita, let me explain," he begged.

"Go fuck yourself," I said. "Don't you have shit to do? I just laid out lots of plans at the club."

"I ain't got shit to do with that, Mamita," he said. "We have to talk. We have to work things out."

"The hell you ain't got shit to do!" I snarled. "And we ain't got to work shit out. Our work is done."

"Baby, be reasonable," he said.

"Done, motherfucker, can't you hear?" I snapped. "And don't ever fucking call me baby again!"

I slammed the door in his face and left him standing there like a dumb-ass, just exactly how he should have been feeling.

CHAPTER TWENTY-THREE

More Money, More Problems

I continued to operate our cartel with the efficiency of the winner on Donald Trump's The Apprentice show. I never mentioned my sex life to the fellas and they never mentioned it again either. But I still felt awkward and uncomfortable about it. I was sure the men talked about their sexcapades all the time. But as a woman, some subjects were still taboo, and I was still a little old-fashioned.

By then, my net worth had skyrocketed to close to two billion dollars. And the combined net worth of the entire cartel approached twenty billion dollars. But it seemed like it was never enough. Captains and lieutenants were greedy, always wanting more and more, always concerned more about my take than their own. I guess that was the hatin' shit in action that Dad had talked about. It just came with the territory.

Along with the haters, being followed by federal agents also came with the territory. They tried to be discreet and nonchalant but I could spot those motherfuckers a mile away. It seemed like everybody was trying to take their best shot at me. If they weren't trying to take away my paper, they were trying to take away my freedom.

That's why I was so focused. I was wired for sound. I had no distractions. But I was in a mood. It had been over a month since I'd gotten any and if that wasn't enough, I thought I might be pregnant. My period was late. So I bought an EPT and sure enough, I was pregnant.

I had been calling Ramos for days to tell him the news. But he didn't answer his phone. I figured that he was afraid I was going to curse him out again. That wasn't the case. I really needed to discuss business with him. Money was drying up along with product. I needed to get more product on the street.

Everything seemed to be happening at once. I guess Biggie didn't lie when he said more money, more problems. I'm a living testament to that.

When it seemed like nothing could get any worse, Carlo showed up at my house at three-thirty one morning. I knew it was an emergency.

"I feel like all of this is my fault," Carlo said as I opened the door.

"Carlo, what are you talking about?"

"I should have never ran my mouth," he said. "I know you don't take any shit, Tammy, but I didn't mean any disrespect. I swear I was just fucking around 'cuz I was drunk."

"Carlo, I still don't have a clue. What is this about?"

"Ramos is gone. And it's all my fault. I knew you were gonna smoke him when you heard me."

"Smoke him? I could never smoke Ramos," I said with sadness. "I love him." It was the first time I was honest with myself. "I'm pregnant with his baby."

I regretted losing control and putting my business out there. But it was too late. There was nothing I could do about it.

"But weren't you mad at him, ma?" he asked.

"Of course I was mad, you dunce," I said. "I was fucking livid. But that doesn't mean I killed him." Carlo gave me a look. "I know I've killed others that made me mad but Ramos was different. He was our connection. That reason in and of itself was enough to let him live."

"Well, I don't know what you're gonna do," he said. "Everyone is gonna think that you did it."

"Thanks for telling me, Carlo," I said and closed the door.

I shuffled over to the couch, curled up into a ball and sobbed, just like I used to do when I was a little girl.

My baby's daddy was dead, I was the suspected killer, and we had no product. The shit had hit the fan and I didn't like the way it looked.

"I swear, Roy! I had nothing to do with it," I said, pleading my case. "I have never been one to lie about what I do. I've always fessed up to everything."

"I don't know why but I believe you," Roy said.

"I believe you too, baby girl."

Dad!

"Now do you see why I asked you to stop being such a hothead, Tamika?" Dad asked. "Some labels get put on you that you can never get rid of. I know and you know that you didn't do it. But what are we supposed to say to the Cubans. You think they're just gonna take our word as law with the disrespect you got from Ramos? You've killed a lot of other people for a lot less."

"You're right, Marley. But I didn't kill him." I was frustrated. "Doesn't that fact mean anything?"

"I wish it did, baby girl," he said. "I wish it did."

Dad and Roy told me to lay low for a little while until they figured out who wanted Ramos dead. I didn't like it, but I did as I was told. Going into hiding left a bad taste in my mouth. I thought it made me look guilty. Running and hiding was not my style at all.

I escaped to a nothing hotel in central New Jersey and spent a lot of time thinking and meditating, trying my damnedest to put two and two together.

But after hours and hours, I couldn't come up with a thing. Ramos was loved by everyone. No one had a reason to kill him. And what was even more frustrating was to the world, I was the only one with a good motive.

Then it finally hit me. Someone was trying to set me up.

I wanted to run my idea past my dad but I was pretty sure he had already thought of it. But there was something I needed to investigate before talking to him anyway. I promised myself that I would leave no stone unturned.

I packed and fell asleep with my forty-five lying safely under my pillow. I was moving out in the morning in search of information. Not knowing was driving me crazy.

CHAPTER TWENTY-FOUR

Tamika Disappears

I needed to go downtown and I needed a disguise. The only way I was going to get answers was to find them on my own. And no one would talk to me if they knew it was me.

So I gave myself a makeover. I didn't even recognize myself! I looked more hoochified than I'd ever looked before, wearing gear that I knew was gonna catch the attention of the person I wanted to reel in.

I drove downtown and found a parking space near where I had to go. I got out of the car and walked two blocks to Fulton Street.

My disguise was a definite success but I hated the catcalls and the 'yo mas' and all the other ignorant shit. If only men knew how to approach a woman.

Anyway, I got the same shit when I rolled up on the set of

my intended target. Of course, his whole crew tried to holla at me. But I had no time to talk to those niggas. I had an agenda, a target—the general of that pathetic small-time operation.

"Hey, Pretty. You sure are looking lovely today," Rodman said. "Do you have a second so I can holla at you?"

"I'm kind of busy right now," I said. "I have to go and get a pedicure."

He said something else but I tuned him out and actually went and got a pedicure. I wasn't in a hurry. I was positive that Rodman's thirsty ass would be right outside waiting for me. I wasn't wrong.

"Do you have time for me now, Pretty?" Rodman asked when I stepped outside the nail salon.

"I'm really kind of busy today," I said. "What's up with you?"

"Everything is up with me. I'm sure you've heard of me. I'm Rodman. I'm a legend in these parts." He was lying his ass off.

"Is that right?" I asked. "So what would a legend like you want with a simple girl like me?"

"I can think of a few things," he said, licking his lips. "A baller like me needs a lady like you on my arm."

"Well, I have a man," I lied. "We may have our problems but he's still my man. I'm not trying to do him dirty like that."

"But, ma, you can't be sweatin' no other small timer when all of this is up in your face," he said. I felt like I was going to puke. "We can make some serious shit happen together."

"So…what can we make happen, Mr. Rodman? That is your name, right?"

"You're a good listener," he said. "The name is Rodman and we can make a lot happen. All you gotta do is believe, Pretty."

"OK. I got a lot of shit to do so let's cut the bull," I said. "I gotta go but you can walk me to my ride if you'd like."

"OK. Now we're getting somewhere," he said. "How far is your car?"

"It's over by the train," I answered. "Do you have the energy to walk over there or are you too ran down to go that far?"

"I like your style," he said. "And I've got mad energy. Walking is not a problem."

"Man, why don't you just drive her," one of his cronies chimed in. "It's hot as shit out here."

"Nigga, will you get out of grown folks' business?" Rodman snapped. "Obviously the lady wants to walk or she would've asked for a ride." He turned to me and put out his arm. "Shall we?"

I humored Rodman and let him lock his arm in mine as

we walked to my ride. All the way there, he laid all kinds of bullshit on me that I was one hundred percent positive wasn't true. I breathed a tremendous sigh of relief when we got to my ride.

I opened the doors with the remote and told him to get in the passenger side. He slid in and adjusted the seat for his long legs. I got in as well and locked the doors.

"Damn, girl! What kind of freaky shit are you into?" he asked when he saw the length of heavy chain on the back seat.

"Oh, don't worry about that," I said. "You can do me a favor, though."

"What's that?" he asked all excited, as if I was about to let him do something to me.

"Can you grab something out the glove box?"

"What would that be?" he asked, opening the box before I had a chance to respond. He pulled out a pair of handcuffs and smiled. So did I.

"What are these for?" he asked seductively.

"I want you to lock one cuff to the chain in the back there and the other one to your left wrist," I instructed, losing my phony accent a little bit with each word.

"Do I know you?" he asked

"Nigga, don't act dumb," I said, pulling my forty-five out of my purse. "Say you don't know that it's me. Tammy."

"Why you look so different? And what the fuck is up with

the heat?"

"I like heat," I said calmly. "Now, just do what I asked. Cuff the chain. Cuff yourself. Chop chop, nigga, chop chop."

"I don't know what this is about," he said while cuffing himself, "but this is some type of misunderstanding."

"Misunderstanding or not, I have some shit I need to get to the bottom of and you're gonna help me."

He looked dumfounded but didn't say a word. I enjoyed the quiet.

Finally, I stopped at a hotel in Elizabeth, New Jersey. He got out of the car lugging the chain and I nudged him with my gun to the room I had rented that morning. I felt like I was finally about to get some answers.

I didn't really know what I could get out of Rodman. I knew, though, that he was a dumb-ass and I would be able to play him. I wasted no time running game.

"Alright, Rodman. You know what I want," I said. "Spill the beans."

"I don't know what the fuck you're talking about," he said.

I didn't believe him.

"So, you wanna play games, huh?" I asked. "We'll put an end to that."

I called my dad on my cell and put him on speaker phone.

"Dad! I'm sitting here with Rodman. I think he has something he wants to tell us."

"Hold on, baby," Dad said. "I have Roy on the other line."

"Call me back so we can be on a three way?"

"Good idea, Tamika," he said. "Hang up and I'll call you right back."

I hung up and waited. Rodman was looking more than a little uncomfortable. My instincts told me that he knew something and I needed to know what he knew.

Dad called back a few minutes later and once again I prodded Rodman.

"Come on, Mr. Big Man, tell me something," I said. "You're the one that was talking about how you're into everything. So tell me what you heard through the grapevine."

"I ain't heard shit," he snapped.

"Nigga, I think you better watch your mouth," my dad chimed in. "Just because I'm not there, don't think you can get cute with my daughter."

"I ain't gettin' cute, Marley," he said. "I just don't know what she's talking about."

"Oh, nigga, you know something," I said. "Don't bitch up now. Speak your mind. You're the big motherfucking baller so don't act like a chump now."

"I can never be a chump," Marley said.

"So why the cat got your tongue then?" I asked. "Show us how about it you are. Show us you're gully. For real, for real. I hear you ain't shit but a frontin'-ass little bitch."

"Yeah right," he said, sounding pissed. "That's why I showed y'all who's the bitch."

"Showed who?" I asked. "You ain't showed me shit. All I hear is you talking loud and all I see is a lot of hot air coming out of your mouth. But you ain't said shit."

"And I ain't gotta say shit," he said cockily. "I'm still hard."

"Nigga, you're as flaky as a Betty Crocker pie crust," I said. "Frontin' like you're tough. You ain't tough, nigga." I get close up in his grill so there's no misunderstanding that I'm punking him.

"Yeah, OK," he fumed. "That's the same shit Ramos was saying when I smoked his ass. That's right. I put that nigga right outta his misery."

"You hear that Dad? You hear that Roy? This punk-ass nigga is saying he's the one who killed Ramos. This nigga can't even spell murder if he was in a Scrabble game and someone spotted him all six letters."

"You got jokes, sis, don't you?" Rodman said. "But the joke is on you. That's why I mercked that nigga. Y'all walking around here like you so special and shit—like nobody else can be down with y'all. I wanted to prove to y'all that y'all squad is weak. Just like your ass is weak, Tamika, frontin' like you hard, having everybody calling you Tammy and shit. I heard about your trial. You're just a scared little girl."

"Oh, I'm a scared little girl now?" I asked before bashing him with the butt of my gun across the head.

"That don't phase me. Fuck you," he snarled.

"No. That's what your pencil dick ass has always wanted to do but couldn't get the job done."

"You damn right I wanna fuck you. I wanna fuck the shit out of you just like my dad did. That's why I killed your corny-ass boyfriend to get his ass out the way."

"Nigga, I don't fuck with old-ass men," I said. "You must be trippin' if you think somebody got some of this."

"Nah, bitch. I ain't trippin'," Rodman says. "Everybody thinks they know me but y'all don't know me. I could care fucking less about y'all corny-ass crew. The only reason I asked to get down wit' y'all is my dad asked me to. And ever since you murdered him, I told myself I was gonna fuck you just like he did—just like it says in all the transcripts from your trial."

"Wait a minute, motherfucker," Dad yells. "Wait a minute Roy, Tamika. When I was looking into Cappy's background, I had hired a private investigator to get the dirt on him. And I remember now that Cappy had a son named Rodney."

"What? Wait a minute. You're Cappy's son?" I couldn't believe it. "You're Cappy's motherfucking son?" I snarled.

"Tamika! Wait!!!" Dad shouted.

It was too late.

"Bow. Bow. Bow. Bow. Bow."

"Tamika! No! You just killed the evidence. The Cubans may not believe us now."

"But Roy just heard him confess..."

"Still. I've known Roy for over twenty years," Dad said. "They may not believe that he can be impartial. They may think he's so cool with me that he'd lie to protect my daughter. You have to stay in hiding. You have to make yourself disappear for a while. We have to deal with the Cubans."

"I'm tired of hiding, Dad. I want everyone to know the truth."

"The truth is I lost you for over a decade, baby girl, and I'm not about to lose you for a lifetime," he said. "I'm not playing, Tamika. I'm not fucking playing with you. Make yourself disappear. Make yourself disappear. Now!"

CHAPTER TWENTY-FIVE

Tamika Back in Kingston

Once again, my hot head and quick temper got me into trouble. But the last thing I wanted was for Ramos to be killed. I knew what everybody thought. But they didn't really understand us. They didn't know what we had. They didn't know we were having a baby.

While Dad was working on the Cubans, I laid low but I was bored. Yes I was rich, and finding ways to make a dent in the billion dollars I earned was fun. But the game was in my blood. Living any other way would be boring.

I mean, who wouldn't love busting somebody in the mouth if they talked slick or busting a cap in their ass if they talk too slick. I loved the power, being in control, no longer being a victim or a weak little girl.

Yeah, maybe to those who judged me I was evil. But I never hurt anyone who didn't hurt me first. It was like karma.

They deserved what I gave them because they had already given it to me. All in all, I thought I would pass the test in the end. Or at least I hoped.

Dad set me up in Nine Miles, Bob Marley's birthplace. He thought the serenity of the place would mellow me out some and cool off my itchy trigger finger.

Truth be told, I was bored.

The view was beautiful. The place I stayed was high up in the mountains. But I felt like Bin Laden hiding in the hills with every mother looking for him.

And I wasn't even sure why I had to hide. The villagers were so friendly. I had never been to such a friendly place before.

I didn't know it at the time, but my hideaway was owned and operated by Bob Marley's family. I should have guessed it though. My dad loved Bob Marley so much he legally changed his name to Marley. Only a handful of people know Dad's real name, and I'm not one of them.

After nearly two weeks of solitude, I had a surprise visitor. My dad.

He strolled in one afternoon with his long locks of matted, plaited hair. My dad was Rastafarian to the bone, just like Bob Marley was.

"Dem duty shotta police boys used to drive up to my

brothers and cut them hair off in locks. We were an oppressed people who knew that a poor man never vex. Them just pretend that all is good and never show anger."

I giggled at his Jamaican just like I did when I was a little girl. Then I ran to hug him. He had a bag behind his back.

"What do you have there?" I asked and peeked in the bag. "Dad! Vegetable Run Down? You know I'm not a vegetarian. I eat meat!"

I complained a little more but the vegetables cooked in coconut milk were to die for.

"You don't always need to eat meat," he said as he watched me devour the food. I was starving. "Cleanse yourself of the wild cow meat. It'll be good for the baby. And you'll have more peaceful spirits inside of you."

"Dad, what I eat has nothing to do with my temper," I said. "People doing stuff to me is what upsets my temper."

"I cannot believe that you're in the land of the great peaceful brother, Bob Marley, and you haven't learned a thing! Time is longer than rope, girl. The noose is waiting for your neck if you keep living the way you are. Peace is the way. Bob Marley showed us the way. He performed a great concert and got the beloved Michael Manley to shake hands on stage with the snake Edward Seaga when they had the country trenched in war. And he performed after they tried to assassinate him. He didn't fire back. He performed in the name of peace and brotherhood."

"Dad, you know you would not let someone get away with trying to assassinate you," I said.

"Man has to protect himself, this is true," Dad said. "But we don't have to kill our brethren like you kill. Life is more precious than that. Bob Marley taught us that. People teased him all the time when he moved to Trenchtown. They said he and other Rastas cut off body parts of people and carried them around in their bags. Bob Marley was randomly searched by the police all the time. It was unfair. It was cruel. They laughed and smiled but Bob Marley knew not everybody 'who kin dem teet wid u is fren'."

"I know, Dad, people smile in your face and talk behind your back all the time," I said. "That's why I never stop my grind. People respect me."

"There is a difference between respect and fear, Tamika. People won't say things to your face if they fear you. They will resent you and hope for the day they can kill you off. But if they respect you, they will never talk bad about you—even when you are not around.

"Bob Marley and his other Trenchtown people had nothing to lose. So instead of wielding guns, they expressed their frustration and anger through their music. They learned to use their guitars to make a revolution. Bob Marley changed the whole world with his songs. That is power, Tamika. That's a lot more respect than shooting a gun can give you."

Dad continued to get on my case.

"As I said, Bob Marley got Michael Manley and Edward Seaga to shake hands. That was major. Ronald Reagan helped to destroy our country by hand-picking Edward Seaga to run Jamaica. Then he put a war on ganja. Ganja was always a great source of wisdom. Anyway, Manley was for the people and Seaga sold the people out. Bob Marley saw the children dying in the streets over the fighting between their supporters. So he spoke out for peace. He got everyone to get along, just like Roy got the Cubans to get along with the Jamaicans. I need you to take the example of Bob Marley and stop taking the example of the Rude-boys. You can't kill just to kill. You can't kill just for a name. You can't kill for respect. Once you kill too much, every death takes food out of all our mouths. Then pretty soon none of us will eat."

Dad turned away from me with a heavy heart. I could see it. I wish I would've told him that I understood but I couldn't.

Yes, Bob Marley was loved for lots of reasons. But I can't stand in my yard like he did and hand out tens of thousands of dollars. The same people who take money from you are the ones who will talk about you later.

The only thing Dad said that I truly understood was that sometimes you have to make friends before starting an all-out war, like the Jamaicans and the Cubans did.

So that's what dad was doing and what he suggested I learn how to do. I didn't know if I could stand down, though.

I liked being feared. I liked being respected.

But maybe, I thought, *I'll compromise somewhere in the future.*

EPILOGUE

After spending several months in Nine Miles, listening to Bob Marley's music, watching my belly grow with Ramos's child, I realized that the place was beginning to wear off on me.

I spoke to my Dad often about the Rastafarian tenets that he and Bob Marley lived by. And I started to see they had a point.

But my dad didn't make it to the top by being a nice guy. I'm certain he was like me when he was young. He just mellowed out with age. I'm not ready to do that.

Besides, I can't ever fully resign myself to peace. After all I've been through, all my experiences, that would be like giving in. I don't give in.

I will always protect myself if I have to. Hell, I'll always protect myself, period. No one will ever mess with me again.

And in a few months I will protect my baby. And God help the motherfucker who messes with him.

I'm thinking that if there were more women in the world who were strong like me, who commanded respect like I do, who were feared like I am, the world would be a much better place for everybody.

So enjoy the quiet everyone. Tammy is coming.

AFTERTHOUGHT

The preceeding story is a fictional depiction of something that sadly happens every day. Too many of our children are unsupervised, neglected and abused. The end result is they never reach the promise that they were destined to achieve. Their lives take entirely different turns often brutal, socially deviant and perilous.

Hopefully this story will commence a dialogue that in the end helps us to take better care of our children. We have to. We see that they aren't doing too well taking care of themselves.

The author
SIDI

Coming soon…

Tamika
*The Struggle
of a Jamaican Girl
Continues*

By

Sidi

CHAPTER ONE

Marley & Tamika Return to NYC

"Tamika, Tamika! We have to go to town soon," Marley calls to his daughter as he approaches her room. They are renting a house in the same town Bob Marley was born, Nine Miles. "The Tourism Board is hosting on an event in preparation for the big reggae festival in New York City next week."

"Hold on," Tamika whispers into her cell phone and hides it before her father reaches her room. "I wasn't planning on going, Dad," Tamika says. "But if I have to, I'll find something to wear and get ready."

"Why you not ready, Tamika?" Marley asks. "This is very big deal. We have to prepare for the festival."

"I know, Dad," Tamika says. "That's why I'm resting and trying to mellow out. I can't fight everybody when we get back to New York if I'm tired. I'm just trying to get my mind right."

Marley looks at his daughter suspiciously and wonders why she has suddenly decided to listen to what he's been telling her all along.

"Well, you stay then. I'll go to the planning session," Marley says as he backs out of her room, still looking at his daughter suspiciously.

Tamika listens intently as her dad walks down the spiral staircase. When she hears the door open and close, she knows it's safe to resume her conversation.

"Haven't I been good to you, Carlo?" Tamika asks. "Haven't I helped you, and a lot of people who are close to you, eat?"

"Of course you have, Tamika," Carlo says. "What kind of a question is that?"

"I'm just saying that you should be down with me. That's all," Tamika says. "The Columbian cartels smuggle billions of dollars worth of cocaine into the United States. And it doesn't matter that they've bribed bankers, lawyers, judges, cops, federal agents. We're the only ones with the money, power, respect and discipline to move that type of product. We could be legendary, Carlo. Years from now when people tell the real story of how cocaine flooded Harlem, they'll be talking about us. We'll be the Dons. Our faces will be known. Our stories will be told. And why shouldn't it be us? Why shouldn't we benefit from the discounted price that they're selling pure cocaine for? We have to jump on this now before the undisciplined crews fuck it up for everybody. And we can't have that. Can we?"

"So what do you want me to do? Kill off all the rival gangs?" Carlo asks.

"No. Not that," Tamika replies. "That would be like we're looking down on the people beneath us. You should never look down on someone unless you're trying to pick them up. That's where we come in. We train any squad that's willing to work with us. But, at the same time, we have to know that every man who *kin dem teet wid u is not fren.* We have to weed them out. If they smile in our faces but we hear that they're talking shit about us behind our backs, we have to deal with them. Now, I know you've heard some things. I'm just asking you to deal with the people you've heard shit about. Send a fucking message, Carlo. When bodies start falling left and right, everyone will know that the Princess of Harlem is on her way back. I don't want no shit when I get back either. I want every stinking person that I cross paths with to feel thankful that they're still alive. I want you to make the shottas go clap, clap, Carlo. I want there to be no doubt that the streets are ours."

"What does Marley say about all this?" Carlo asks.

"He is my dad, and I love him dearly, but we're not on the same page right now," Tamika says. "He thinks that everyone should hold hands and sing a Bob Marley ballad in unison. Meanwhile, those that are behind us are gaining ground because they're hungrier than we are. You think those people are gonna respect us because we're feeding other people? How can we ask them to not be grimy when they ain't eating off of our plates? A hungry man has to eat, Carlo. So, either they eat with us or we take them out if they don't want to sit at our table. That's all I'm asking you to do. Like Beanie Sigel said in *State Property*, 'Niggas have to either get down or lay down.' I expect you to start that happening before I get there."

"And what do I get out of it?" Carlo asks.

"I swear, Carlo, I mean no disrespect," Tamika says. "I love Roy. He and my dad have been friends for years. He's like a grandfather to me. But he's taking forever to give you a stronger position in the organization. I'm not asking you to step on his toes or anybody else's toes in the organization. I'm just saying that you deserve a leg up. That's what I can give you. You know that I have the money and power to make that happen. I can't do it by myself, though. You're the missing piece like Ramos used to be. So let's join forces and make this happen."

"So, what's my percentage?" Carlo asks.

"Don't worry about that," Tamika says. "You know you're gonna eat. With me, everybody eats."

"True," Carlo says. "Well, I guess I'll get to work then."

Without saying another word Tamika smiles and closes her cell phone. She feels content that she's back in the game.

Carlo chooses several of his grimiest crew members and tells them to grab their heat and meet up with him in Brooklyn at a pool hall on 161st Street.

"There's no other way to say this than to just say it," Carlo says. "We have to take advantage of the money being left on the table. I haven't been eating enough lately, and I'm more than hungry. So we're going to soften the streets up then partake of some of that good shit the Columbians just brought in. Then maybe the hunger pangs will go away."

"Not to go against what you're saying because I love to play war games," says power player, Hannibal. "But after we bust some heads open, how will we be able to afford to partake in that Columbian shit? They're dealing in heavy weight only. We could all chip in everything we have and still fall short."

Hannibal is five feet nine inches tall with a bald head and massive shoulders. He's so muscular that people kid him all the time about not having a neck. Despite being able to break someone in half using just his bare hands and the force behind his two hundred eighty pound frame, Hannibal fancies a Colt .45 revolver to do his dirty work. He's a beast just like Hannibal Lector.

"Good question, Hannibal," Carlo answers. "But don't sweat it because we have help." The group looks at Carlo curiously. "The Princess of Harlem is about to come home."

"Word? Tamika?" Hannibal asks.

"Yeah, Tamika," Carlo says. "And you know how she's living."

"Hell, yeah! We get to wild the fuck out now," Hannibal says giving pounds and shaking hands with the other crew members.

"That's right," Carlo says. "Go out into the streets, shooting first and asking questions later. If there's anybody you're suspicious about, just take his ass out! Take out his entire fucking crew if you have to. But if you think that a crew would benefit from our guidance and we would benefit from them, let those motherfuckers live. We have to get at this paper. And we have less than a week before Tamika gets here. Let's make her feel welcome. And let's make sure that she doesn't change her mind about backing us financially."

"Yeah, 'cause we need that," Hannibal says with a grin. He heard the story about how Tamika gave everyone on her crew a million dollar sign-on bonus and definitely wants a piece of that action.

Hannibal and Li'l Timmy sit in a gypsy cab on 111th St. in Harlem. They're spying on a sheisty dealer with a bad gambling habit by the name of Bingo.

"How long are you going to be?" asks the driver.

"Chill the fuck out," Li'l Timmy barks. "I gave you a hundred dollars and we ain't been in your cab five fucking minutes yet."

Li'l Timmy is four foot six, a midget with an overwhelming Napolean complex. But, in his case, his bark is not bigger than his bite.

You will rarely ever see Li'l Timmy without his nine millimeter pistol and steel tipped, cop-killer bullets. And everyone knows that with Li'l Timmy's temper, it doesn't take much for him to whip out his gun and pull the trigger.

Li'l Timmy and Hannibal are stalking Bingo, waiting for the best opportunity to ambush him.

"Why do we have to wear these masks?" Hannibal asks, tossing one at Timmy. "If somebody sees us and tells the Jakes that a big-ass nigga and a midget did this, who the fuck do you think they're gonna pin it on? Everybody knows we hang together. It's better to be straight gangsta and look everyone in the eye after we do it. That's the best way to let motherfuckers know that they'd better keep their damned mouths shut."

"You's one straight gangsta-ass, nigga," Li'l Timmy says.

"Why, thank you very much," Hannibal replies. "You ain't so bad yourself."

As Hannibal and Li'l Timmy watch Bingo, a couple of guys walk up to him. They pull out wads of money, waving the bills in the air, then throw a pair of dice against the wall.

Bingo laughs and reaches into his pocket to pull out his own wad of bills. Then he picks up the dice, has a few words with the two guys, and throws them into the wall.

A few more words are exchanged before all three men start throwing their money on the ground. Bingo shakes the dice in his hand and throws them again. He's trying to hit his number.

Hannibal taps Li'l Timmy on the shoulder and nods his head in the direction of Bingo. Then he opens the cab door and steps out. Li'l Timmy does the same.

"Don't go nowhere," Li'l Timmy says to the driver. "We'll be right back."

Li'l Timmy leaves his door open for a quick getaway, and together he and Hannibal walk towards Bingo.

"Time's up, Bingo," Hannibal growls.

Bingo barely has time to turn around before the butt of the .45 smashes into his face.

He hollers in pain, and the two other gamblers take a giant step back and get out of the way.

"That's right," Li'l Timmy says. "You can kiss the motherfucking baby good-bye."

"What's this about?" Bingo stutters.

"Your next-in-command can ask us that after you're gone," Hannibal says.

Buck. Buck. Buck. Buck. Buck.

Hannibal and Li'l Timmy shoot Bingo up in broad daylight and then calmly turn and stroll back to the cab.

The block watches in horror and amazement as Bingo bleeds out onto the sidewalk. Hannibal and Li'l Timmy can't actually be that bold, can they?

Yes they can. And so is the rest of Carlo's hand-picked crew.

Over a four day period, that same scenario repeats itself over and over again in Harlem, Brooklyn and the Bronx like a scene out of *Groundhog's Day*. The end result is over a hundred minor and mid-level players are taken out, in both broad daylight and at night.

It doesn't take long for players in all the boroughs of New York to get nervous. And, just as she desired, Tamika returns to the safe haven she demanded.

CHAPTER TWO

Marley Regains His Notoriety

Father and daughter land at John F. Kennedy International Airport after a long and grueling flight. But as they emerge from Customs, it is apparent that something has happened. Marley is treated like royalty. The uncomfortable trip quickly becomes a distant memory.

"Hello, sir," strangers say as he passes.

Marley's confidence in the fact that his reputation has remained intact grows. But he's totally unaware that a good portion of the goodwill he's receiving is due to Tamika's master plan to soften up the streets.

"Well, Dad, I guess you're still the man," Tamika says, stroking his ego. "Just look at the way they're treating you."

"That's only because I haven't been around in a while," Marley says. "Believe me, it'll wear off in time."

Tamika doesn't comment. She knows her dad well

enough to know that, even though he's being modest, he's basking in all of the attention.

There's hope for him after all, Tamika thinks.

Marley heads straight for the Jamaican Embassy after dropping his luggage off at the Waldorf Astoria.

Tamika has other plans, though, and wants no part of the old-school festival. She says that she is going to rest, but as soon as her dad leaves, she's meeting up with her squad.

Tamika waits in the lobby for Carlo. Ordinarily, she would take a gypsy cab but prefers to get a feel for the scene again before taking any risks. She's been gone a while.

Carlo pulls up in a Hummer and all Tamika can do is chuckle and shake her head. She runs outside and hops in, hugging Carlo over the gear shift.

"Carlo, good to see you!" Tamika says. "But didn't you learn anything from Frank Lucas about keeping a low profile?"

"What are you talking about? The Hummer?" Carlo asks. "I'm not driving this for that reason. This is the real deal. They drive these in wars and shit. The metal is hard as shit, the glass is bulletproof. I just had it waxed up real nice for you, too."

"If say so," Tamika says.

"For real, I'm not flossing," Carlo says. "I don't want you to blame me when you say people ain't eating."

"It's cool. Forget about it," Tamika says. "Is everybody together?"

"Yeah. They're waiting for us at the spot in Brooklyn," Carlo says.

"Good," Tamika replies. "I want to look my entire new squad in the eyes before I get too deeply in bed with them."

"Well, they're all looking forward to seeing you," Carlo says.

"True that," Tamika replies.

Tamika walks into the bar on 161st with Carlo to a standing ovation.

"Princess, it's good to see you," they say.

"It's good to see all of you, too," Tamika replies. "But sit down. I ain't that special. You are the ones who need to be commended. I can tell that you've put in mad work out there in the streets. Niggas have been acting like it's the nineteen-sixties, and they can't look us in the eyes when we approach them."

"We heard that's the way you wanted it, ma," Hannibal says.

"You heard right, and that's exactly how it is," Tamika says. "I'm proud of you. You sure know how to make a bitch want to tear up and shit."

"Yeah, right, Tamika," Carlo says. "Like you're ever gonna cry."

"I can cry," Tamika says. "I cried when they killed Ramos." Tamika looks around to make sure everyone believes her. "I cried when I had the miscarriage and lost his baby. I have emotions like everybody else."

"Well, it's about to be all happy," Hannibal says.

"You can believe that," chimes in Li'l Timmy.

"So, Carlo, are you going to introduce me to everybody?" Tamika asks.

"Of course," Carlo says, standing up. "The big guy and little guy are Hannibal and Li'l Timmy." He points them both out. "They get into so much shit together that we tease them and call them a married couple. But don't get it fucked up. If you want havoc, you couldn't pick a better team to make it happen.

"This right here is John Carlo, our Italian assassin," Carlo continues. "You know, every crew needs its token Italian."

"Fuck you very much," John Carlo says.

"You're welcome," Carlo replies.

"This is Robert, Trusty, Stanley, Truth, Pete-Pete, Manny, Roger, Chris, Red Dot, and Amazon," Carlo says as he points to each person around the room.

Tamika exchanges pleasantries with all of them, then mentally prepares to fill them in on as many specifics as she's comfortable discussing. But first, she wants to stroke their egos a little more.

"I wasn't kidding when I told you how impressed I am," Tamika says. "My father felt so good while he was walking through the airport that he may consider playing a bigger roll in the organization."

"Damn! Marley?" Carlo remarks. "That would be huge."

"That's what I saw in his eyes," Tamika says.

As she tells the group what she thinks they want to hear, Marley meets with the heads of the Unity of Jamaican Brothers at the Jamaican embassy to reclaim his position at the head of the table.

"Hello, gentlemen. I'm back," Marley says from the head of the oval conference table. "And before I go any further, I need to make sure that none of you has a problem with my being in charge."

No one says a word. They all want to eat off of Marley's plate.

"My daughter has softened up the entire city for us," Marley says. "She's such a fucking hothead sometimes. She doesn't even know that I know what she's been up to. But nothing gets by me. At times, we'll need her level of ruthlessness. But don't worry. I can control my daughter. She still answers to me. And we will get a big piece of that Columbian cocaine pie. You can believe that."

Marley continues laying down the law to the UOJB as they listen intently. When he feels he's said enough for one day, he wraps things up.

He hails his limousine driver once he's back outside. Coming back to America has made him feel special. And he's soaking it in. He gets into the limousine as if he's royalty.

As old and wise as Marley is, he could learn a lot from

his daughter. A limousine ride would be something Tamika would consider too risky. But Marley has been gone too long to be aware of all the new perils of the street.

If he had a crew with him, someone would have easily spotted the green Ford Explorer with Jersey plates following the limo.

Tamika returns to the Waldorf and goes directly to her suite. She thinks of a lie to tell her father about where she's been but notices that she doesn't need to. She's beaten him back.

The day's events were so satisfying that all she wants to do is relax and enjoy it.

She runs the bath, dribbling in the fragrant bubble bath supplied by the Waldorf, pops open a bottle of Cristal and pours a glass. She then loads a CD into the stereo and presses play.

Tamika tests the water with her toes and slips into it. The temperature is perfect. She leans her head against the terry covered inflated pillow on the far end of the tub and reaches for the glass of Cristal.

"And nothing even matters at all," she sings along with Lauren Hill.

Knock, knock, knock.

"Fuck! It never fails," Tamika whines upon hearing the knock at the door. "Every time I try to relax, something interrupts me. No wonder I'm no good at chilling out."

Tamika gets up and grabs a robe. She places it around her wet body and steps into her slippers.

"Coming!" she calls out as she walks toward the door.

Tamika peers out the peephole and sees the same harmless looking white man who that greeted Marley and her when they first arrived. Feeling reassured, she opens the door.

"I have a package for Tamika Jefferson," says the concierge with a smile.

"Thanks. I wonder who this is from," Tamika says. "I'll bring you a tip when I come down later."

"That's fine, ma'am," the concierge says before tipping his hat and walking away.

Tamika looks at the package as she places it on the table. She hesitates before picking it up and shakes it. Nothing rattles around.

Her curiosity gets the better of her so she goes into her luggage and pulls out a pair of cuticle scissors. She uses them to cut away the packaging tape and rips into the box.

"Noooooooooooooooooooooooooooooooo!" Tamika wails when she looks inside.

She crumbles to the floor, hysterically sobbing and screaming. Ten minutes later, the hotel's assistant manager knocks at her door.

"Ma'am, is everything alright in there?"

Tamika doesn't respond.

He looks at the desk clerk he has brought with him and shakes his head at her.

"Use your key," he says. "We have to go in and find out what's going on."

She opens the door to find Tamika kneeling on the carpet, rocking back and forth, still making way too much noise for the staid hotel.

They approach her in an attempt to console her. But, before they reach her, the desk clerk can't help but look at the contents of the box.

"Oh my God!" she gasps.

The assistant manager peers into the box and sees Marley's head, hands, tongue and a foot, raggedly sliced and bloody, and promptly faints.

The desk clerk, however, doesn't panic. She picks up the phone, calls the head of security and instructs him to call the police. Then she kneels besides Tamika and tries to comfort her. But Tamika is beyond being comforted by a simple hug. She wants vengeance. Revenge will be her ultimate comfort.

I'm going to kill any motherfucker who even looks like they had something to do with this, Tammy thinks.

No one yet knows it, but Tamika is gone. Tammy has taken control. And anything is bound to happen.

Also by

Sidi…

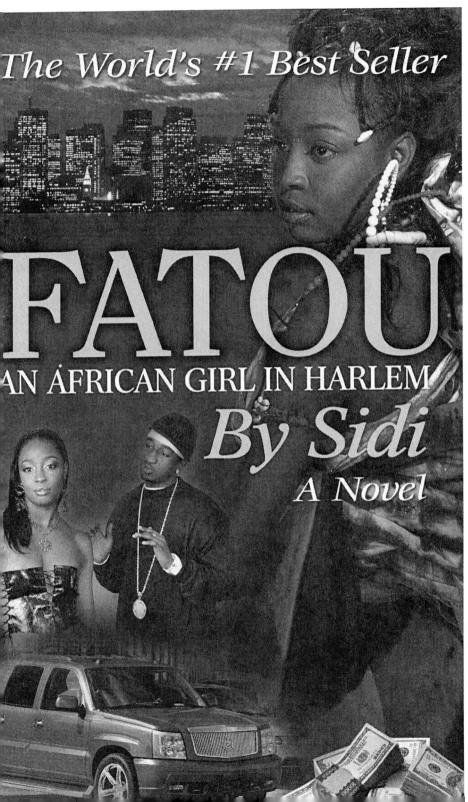

Fatou
An African Girl in Harlem

Twelve year old Fatou travels from West Africa to America thinking she's furthering her education. Yet, she arrives in New york City greeted by a man three times her age— someone from her village who paid a dowry to be her husband. Suffering through pedophiles, deplorably cruel living conditions, and a slave-life job eventually pushes her over the edge. When the smoke clears, she refuses to be a victim and exerts control of her life by becoming part of Harlem's fast money scene. The resulting terror leveled at anyone who gets in her way doesn't mask her old wounds but it does soothe her overwhelming hunger for revenge. Aside from money,power,respect,and her new love for New York city's number one drug lord, that's all a West African girl in Harlem has to look forward to.

This fast paced novel examines what happens when the bonds of family and tradition fall apart. And it shows how a strong and fearless woman can hold her own surrounded by grimey men in the dangerous drug game.

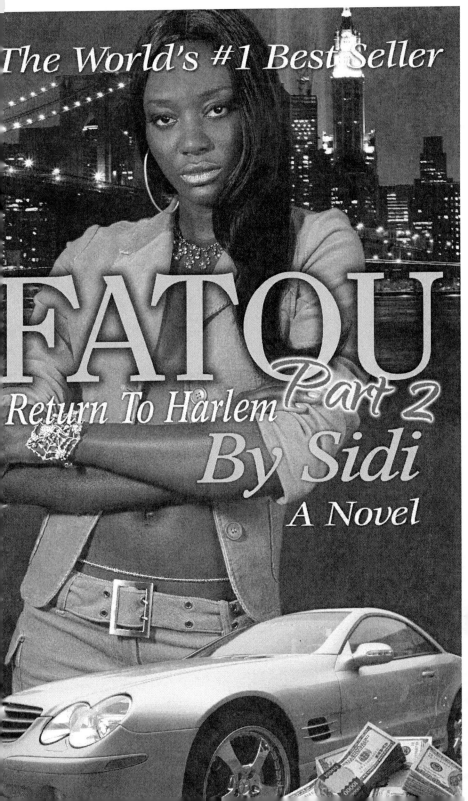

The World's #1 Best Seller

FATOU
Part 2
Return To Harlem
By Sidi
A Novel

Fatou Part 2
Return to Harlem

With the love of her life mysteriously murdered, West African Harlemite Fatou sets out to discover- which of her murdered lover's lieutenants in New York City's most notorious drug cartel was responsible for setting him up. After finally getting to a peaceful state in her own life despite suffering through pedophilia, rape, being kidnapped, and working under slave labor type wages, the death of the man that picked her up when she was down finally pushes Fatou over the edge. And, although the lieutenants mistakenly assume that the death of Fatou's lover will soften the reigns of her control, they find out that he was the one that had previously cooled her down when she was about to blast off. There will be no such luck now that Fatou is on her own and poised to exact revenge. Everyone around her will find out what happens when a woman with an attitude is in control and determined to get respect one beat down at a time.

The rage in this story of revenge is furious and shows you that you'd be better off antagonizing a ravenous pit-bull than to get on the wrong side of the wrong woman. Beware everyone because Fatou is back with a vengeance. I advise everyone to duck, put down your shades, and close your curtains. Don't be caught in the path of her wrath.

MANDINGO
THE GOLDEN BOY

By SIDI

AUTHOR OF FATOU, FATOU 2 AND THE LESBIAN'S WIFE

PROLOGUE

Denise Jackson
January 2003

Although I'd been with boys before in high school, that's just what they were—boys. And none of them had the length and girth of the grown-ass man standing in front of me. I swear to God, he has to be longer than a ruler and wide enough to fuck up some of my internal shit. Still, I have to go through with this. That's the only way I'm gonna know if he'll be to women what I am to men—the best damned sex money can buy.

I'm scared to ask him to continue taking his clothes off. The bulge in his boxers is very impressive, and I'm afraid his dick is gonna spring out and knock me into the wall or something. To allay my fears, I try to concentrate on a different part by turning my attention to the rest of his body.

The muscles ripping out of his chest and arms make him look like a Mr. Universe contestant. Yet he's not so diesel that it's a turn-off. His six-pack stomach and his thighs are so lean and developed he could race against a horse. He's a strong stallion, alright. The stud-muffin every woman dreams about but never has the chance to experience. I'm about to audition him to make sure he's capable of making their wildest dreams come true. Well, at least those women who can afford him.

"Do you want me to take these off?" he asks in a heavily accented voice.

I feel the lump in my throat grow larger.

"Sure, sweetie," I answer as calmly as I can. "Where'd you say you were from? Africa?" I ask him even though I already know the answer.

"I am from the Mandingo tribe," he replies proudly.

"Nigga, you ain't never lied!"

As he pulls his boxers down, I see it's going to be worse than I thought. He's got a good twelve inches and he's only half hard.

Goddamn! I say to myself. *Some serious fucking is about to go down.*

PART ONE

Looking Back

Through the eyes of Mandingo, Denise, & Moriba
January 2003 to December 2002
Harlem, New York

CHAPTER ONE

Mandingo

As Denise steps out of her dress revealing a silky Victoria's Secret chemise, all my problems become irrelevant. All that matters to me are the ample breasts straining to stay inside her negligee. Her thighs are thicker than those of any of the pale faces that walk the halls of Columbia University and her butt is a sight for sore eyes. I look up into the air and thank Allah for also giving Denise the brains to make it into one of the toughest schools in America.

I've been lusting after Denise since she befriended me a year ago when I first arrived here. I guess the connection that blacks in America have with each other kicked in when she saw me. Back then, she didn't know I was African. I guess all she cared about was that I was one of the few dark faces in the lily-white crowd. I didn't care what the reason was, though. All that mattered to me was that she was the prettiest woman I'd ever seen in my life and she was talking to me. Just a few words and I was making plans for our wedding and honeymoon, especially our honeymoon.

Regrettably for me, I learned that there were a few problems with the plans I was making for Denise. First and foremost, she is what Americans call a carpet-muncher, meaning that she is attracted to other women. That difficulty alone loomed largely enough but, additionally, her occupation was another disqualifying factor. To put it bluntly, she was a high priced call girl, and I was a broke college student. We were definitely not a match made in heaven.

Even though Denise and I became close, I always beat her upside her head with questions about why with all that she had going for herself would she still decide to degrade herself by selling her body. She'd always say, "You're my boy but your broke-ass is just like all those other niggas trying to get some pussy for free." She had a point, but I still wasn't wrong. There are a million things a woman can do besides prostituting herself. All it takes is a little hard work.

Damn. Now I feel like a hypocrite. I'm talking all of that trash about Denise but the only reason she's about to give me some is because she wants to make sure I'll please the rich clients she has lined up for me. But hell, any excuse to be with this bombshell is good enough for me. She has a body like Vivica Fox and a face like Stacey Dash. Allah forgive me for the illicit acts I'm about to commit but I don't know a man who's strong enough to withstand her charms. I'm so glad Karen Steinberg told her about our little run-in.

Karen was a country girl from Kentucky who put the C, O, U, N, T, R, and Y in the word. I swear if you look in Webster's you'll see a picture of her smiling face right next to country. But I ain't mad at her though.

For one, she's one of the smartest people to ever graduate from high school in her state. How else do you think she got here? Poor white trash can't afford this place just like we can't.

The other reason I ain't mad at her is she looks like a blond- haired, blue-eyed Daisy Duke. Keep it real. Your eyes are glued to the TV, too, whenever you can catch the Dukes of Hazard reruns on Spike TV. What man wouldn't be lusting after Daisy Duke? Not to say that I was lusting after Karen Steinberg, but I noticed her.

Karen Steinberg has breasts similar to Denise's and long, flowing legs. She's pretty much the classic white bombshell. Kinda tall and slim with big titties. She does have a little phatty for a white girl. Yet, still, like I said, I wasn't all big on her. She stepped to me.

I was in the cafeteria one day when she came in. A couple of the resident loudmouths started talking trash to her after she grabbed her food so I motioned for her to sit with me. I guess I just felt bad for her. And I knew that the only reason they were clowning with her in the first place was because she wouldn't sleep with any of them. Nevertheless, I was certain that they would calm that shit down once she sat with me and I wasn't wrong. Soon as Karen Steinberg's ass hit the chair all of her hecklers became quiet as church mice. The resulting silence gave us the perfect opportunity to hold our own little private conversation.

Karen wanted to know what it was like in Africa. She asked if we still ran around hunting bears with spears. Although I thought that was an ignorant, racist question, I also found it amusing that those myths still exist.

I didn't answer her. Instead, I asked her if she still wrestled pigs in the slop pen. She started laughing. I guess she got my point because she changed the subject.

She asked me why blacks got mad about some myths and were quick to cling to others. Of course I didn't know what she meant so I asked her to be more specific. Her response made me fall out.

She said, "You got mad that I asked you if you were a hunter but if I had asked you if you had a big, African dick, instead, you would have been quick to agree with me."

After I finished laughing, I said, "That's because your first assumption was ridiculous and your second is true."

"Yeah, right," she said. "Everyone knows the myth about black guys being bigger than white guys. It's legend."

"Nah, baby girl, it's an actual fact," I said proudly.

"Well, show me," she replied.

"What? You can't be serious."

"I'm dead serious," she said, unaware that that was the beginning of the end for her.

We went back to my dorm room and I put on some reggae. I thought Shabba Ranks was appropriate for the moment.

I started gyrating my body to the rhythms of Shabba as I undressed. I could tell that she was more than impressed with my body. After watching her stare at my chest and arms, I decided to rub some baby oil on them to make them glisten. I planned to intensify whatever pleasure this naive white girl was feeling as she lusted over my African features. And, truth be told, she had no idea what the fact of my being of the Mandingo tribe meant. She was definitely about to find out.

When I finally got down to taking off my boxers she gasped. "Is that thing real?" she asked.

I grabbed her arm and pulled her to me.

"Come on over here, girl, and find out."

She started stroking my dick while she kissed my neck. I could feel myself starting to elongate. Soon I would be at my full fifteen inches.

I smiled when her kisses went from my chest to my stomach. She looked in amazement at my python and muttered repeatedly, "Oh my God."

"Don't pray to Jah now, baby girl," I said. "Your mouth got you into all of this trouble you're in."

I got tired of playing with Karen Steinberg so I finally grabbed the top of her shoulders and guided her down to her knees.

"So, what are you going to do with this big African dick?" I asked her. Without responding, she showed me.

Believe me when I tell you, the myth about white girls knowing how to suck a golf ball through a straw is not a lie. Come to think of it, a redneck, country-ass white girl has even more skills than a regular one. I didn't know that then, but I do now. But I'll tell you about that later. Let me get back to Karen Steinberg and her talented mouth.

At first, she kissed the tip. It was like a series of quick pecks on the lips. But instead of it being my lips, it was the round, sensitive head of my dick.

Out of nowhere, she glanced up at me with the most devilish grin I've ever seen then she took the plunge. She skillfully took me inside her mouth and wrapped her lips around my dick as if she was giving it a bear hug. All the while, she stared deeply into my eyes.

There's something about a woman looking in your eyes while she's pleasuring you orally. It's a reassurance that lets you know that she knows exactly what she's doing and who she's doing it to. And she was doing it to death.

She bobbed her head up and down as her mouth made slurping sounds each time she swished her tongue.

"Suck that big African dick!" I demanded, encouraging her.

I doubt that she needed my encouragement, though. She was already going to town.

When her oral prowess started to feel too good, I wanted her to stop. I wasn't going to let her get away with just a Lewinsky. I wanted to pound her white pussy for all it was worth, especially because of the dumb shit she said to me earlier.

"Are you ready for me to ruin that white hole?" I asked.

She started shaking her head and mumbling through slurps on my dick. Yet, that wasn't enough for me. I wanted to hear her speak in plain English.

I pulled my dick out of her mouth roughly and started smacking her in the face with it.

"Beat me with that black dick, Mandingo," she said while catching her breath. "Beat me with it."

I had never understood why my uncle Moriba cheated on his wives even though he had three of them and therefore shouldn't have been bored with any of them. But as I was severely degrading and disrespecting Karen Steinberg, the reasons started to become clear to me.

I would never be seriously involved with Karen Steinberg. But she's a master at sucking dick so I wouldn't mind letting her do it to me again. I just didn't want her to feel like I thought she was special.

She had given me some oral sex that made me go berserk. And I was about to get some white pussy for the first time. I didn't care about Karen Steinberg so I told myself I could do whatever I wanted to her without explaining myself. She really didn't fucking matter to me then. So I fucked the shit out of her that day.

Karen Steinberg was every man's fantasy—a piece of ass you could do whatever the hell you wanted to with none of the bitching and moaning you usually had to deal with. She was the perfect "other woman" to me. She could have been any of the women my uncle Moriba cheated on his wife with. But that day, she was my first victim at Columbia.

After smacking her repeatedly in the face with my dick, I was finally ready to fuck her.

"Turn around," I yelled at her.

"You're too big for that way," she said with pleading eyes.

"I'm just a man about to prove that certain myths are not myths. Just turn the fuck around and take what I'm about to give to you."

Karen Steinberg remained on her knees while she turned around slowly...cautiously...deliberately.

I paused to stare briefly, somewhat in awe at how nice her ass was for a white girl, round and plump. It definitely wasn't a wide board butt like other white chicks. It poked out just the way I like it.

After putting on a Magnum condom, I nudged forward to tease her with the tip for a moment. She rocked back eagerly. I knew that wouldn't last for long though. Her ass was about to run for the hills when I really started giving her the dick.

For fifteen minutes, I gave it to her an inch at a time. As every minute passed, I gave her another inch. By the time it reached ten minutes, she was ready to pass out. I was having none of that, though. I smacked her ass really hard until it turned red. I giggled to myself, pleased at how it wiggled like jelly. She looked back at me speechless. I could tell that she wanted to holler or scream or moan or at least tell me to stop smacking her ass so hard. My dick must have been killing her. Her breaths were caught somewhere in her throat. She wasn't able to make the minutest of sounds.

After I had made her take all of me, I started growing bored with the silence. I decided it was time to make Karen Steinberg get a sore throat.

I braced myself carefully behind her and grabbed her small waist tightly with both hands. I rammed myself into her as hard as I could. With each thrust I got more turned on by the way her ass was jiggling. Not to mention her whimpering had me really feeling myself. But it was still not enough.

I rocked back enough to totally remove myself from her then thrust myself back in. She let out a loud shriek.

At that point, I knew I had her where I wanted her so I started repeating the process of taking my dick out and thrusting it back in.

"Oh shit, Mandingo! Goddamn. Oh my damn. Fuck!"

Karen Steinberg was shouting out combinations of curse words I'd never heard before.

Yeah I thought, *I'm wearing her ass out.*

I had no idea about Karen Steinberg's previous sex partners. But I will say that she had one of the tightest pussies I ever had. At the time, I thought that she was so tight because white men have little dicks. My experiences with other white girls after Karen Steinberg clued me in that it wasn't true. It was just her. With that little-ass pussy, I must have been killing her.

I rammed my dick in and out of Karen Steinberg for about ten minutes until her shit started to get to me. Then I put the whole thing inside of her and started grinding it as deep as I could. If I remember correctly, I think I felt my dick hit her kneecap. I don't fucking know how and I know I didn't care. All that mattered to me at the time was that she had some good-ass pussy.

I can't even say that her shit was good for a white girl. She could have been red, black, green or orange, it didn't matter. Her shit was popping. It may have been the best shot in my life. That's why I kept fucking her even after that night. And I'm glad she wanted more. I thought it would just be one and done after I degraded her the way I did.

When I felt myself getting ready to come, I pulled out of Karen Steinberg and pulled the rubber off. She sighed as if she felt instant relief then I started smacking her in the face with my dick again. Eventually, I shoved it in her mouth and started barking out commands.

"Suck this big, black dick you white whore," I yelled at her. "Suck it," I repeated over and over as she obliged me.

After a couple of slurps from her talented mouth, I think I shot a gallon of come into her mouth while holding the back of her head to ensure that she didn't move. Once the last drop came out, I relaxed and slumped backwards.

She started gagging like a five hundred pound man was choking her with both hands. Then she ran to the sink and continued to gag while simultaneously spitting into the sink. Finally, she stomped over to me and preceded to tear me a new asshole.

"You have some fucking big-ass balls, you freakin' African," she screamed. "Some big-ass balls."

"What the fuck is wrong with you?" I asked, pretending to be totally oblivious to her issue.

"You fucking come in my mouth? That's what you do? You fucking come in my mouth?"

"What do you mean?" I said. "If you weren't cool with it, why the hell did you let me finish? You should have pulled away."

"No. You should have pulled away like any other man who had some fucking respect for me would have done."

"But you liked it…"

"I liked it?" she said interrupting me. "You think I fucking liked it?"

"Yeah. That's what white girls do. Black girls front like they don't like it, but white girls will gladly swallow your cum."

"Well, this one won't," she yelled, scurrying around looking for her clothes.

Once I realized she was serious, I apologized over and over. But she wasn't beat.

"No, you meant to disrespect me, Mandingo, so why should I accept your apology?"

"Because I really am sorry."

"You're not sorry. If you were sorry, why did you laugh at me then?"

I'd almost forgotten that I had laughed. The whole situation was so fucking unexpected it caught me off guard. I didn't think she heard me. Still, I wasn't laughing at her. I was laughing at the situation. And even she had to admit it, it was a funny-ass situation.

Who starts gagging like that after you take your dick out of their mouth?

At any rate, I didn't tell her what I was thinking. She probably wouldn't have looked at things the same way as I did anyway.

Surprisingly, we were able to peace everything up that night. Or so I thought. To this day, Karen Steinberg stills mentions the time she says I disrespected her.

That night, though, after sulking for what seemed an eternity, she started complaining about not having an orgasm.

"How could you say that?" I asked. "You were screaming your fucking lungs out."

"I was screaming because I was in pain, you asshole, not because it felt good."

Karen Steinberg's words hit me like an unexpected sucker punch. But it wasn't because I was so big on her. I thought hard about what she said. Other women in my life had screamed like hell, too. I always thought that my dick was the bomb to them. But apparently I had the game totally fucked up.

"If I was hurting you, Karen, why didn't you say so?"

MANDINGO: THE GOLDEN BOY *BY SIDI*

I finally asked.

"Why should I?" she replied. "Your intention was to show me that black men have bigger dicks than white men and that you did. What reason did I have to just give up the fight before it even started?"

"All I know is that if someone is hurting you then you let them know. Hell, if it was a sister she would have said something," I said, trying more to convince myself than her.

"That's what you think, Mandingo, but you're wrong," she said sweetly. "Trust me, you're not just big because you're black. You're big for any man. And any woman who's had some of that big-ass dick was in pain. They were probably just too proud to tell you."

Out of nowhere Karen Steinberg started smiling.

"Correction. They probably didn't want to further inflate your already humongous ego."

"I'm not conceited."

"No one is saying you're conceited, but you do have a big-ass ego. Let a woman compliment you sometimes. You don't always have to give yourself props."

Clearly, my dick had Karen Steinberg talking crazy that night but her words did put a heart into what had previously just been some nice titties and a plump ass. Plus, I was still kinda upset about her not having an orgasm.

"Did I ever tell you that you're smart, Karen Steinberg?" I asked.

"I guess I should be worried," she said. "You're complimenting me. What the hell do you want?"

"Why do I have to want something?" I asked.

"Because men always do," she said. "They treat you like shit on a regular basis because they want something. Then they act like you're the fucking queen of England."

"Well, regardless if I want something or not, I've honestly always thought you were smart. Why else would you be here?"

Karen Steinberg never answered me. She just rested her head on my shoulders.

"I'm still turned on," she had said. "My pussy is sore as all hell, but I'm still turned on. Do you think you can finish the job without trying to kill me?"

Without answering, I pulled her over to me and started kissing her neck. Before long, I started hungrily sucking on her titties.

It's baffling to me why I hadn't touched her titties before despite being so big on them. I guess she was right about me not caring about her. I'm not sure I ever started caring. But I was sure that I didn't like the fact that she didn't come. I remember thinking that the only way I was leaving that night without her having an orgasm was in a body bag.

After sucking on her titties long enough to get hard again, I laid on top of her and eased myself into her. She wrapped her legs around my back and we started grinding together in rhythm.

"Yes, Mandingo," she moaned. "This is how you're

supposed to give a girl some of this big-ass dick."

I have to admit, it felt a lot better doing it slowly and carefully than it did acting like I was running a hundred yard dash.

She let me lead for a while then she asked me to let her get on top. I didn't care. As long as she didn't ask me to stop. I was possessed by the thought of making her come wildly and crazily.

Wildly and crazily, it's funny I use those words. That's exactly how Karen Steinberg started acting.

When she got on top, she started grinding on me like she was riding a horse. It was kind of exotic. But it wasn't anything to write home bragging about. Then something changed. She started moaning really loud and hopping up and down harder and harder on my dick.

"Yes, Mandingo," she shouted. "Fuck me with this big black dick! Fuck the shit out of me you motherfucker!"

Karen Steinberg really started wilding out. She was bouncing on me like she was crazy. She grabbed a handful of my chest with her nails and was pounding me into the bed. It's a good thing I didn't have a girlfriend at the time or I would have been in trouble. I didn't care, though. The shit was starting to feel real good. And the way Karen Steinberg was acting was turning me the fuck on.

Before I had a chance to come the second time, Karen Steinberg let out a really loud shriek then slammed her pussy down hard on every inch of my dick. I could feel her pussy pulsating around my dick and before long she started to shake. Her eyes got really big and she became extremely quiet with the exception of her heart beating like an African drum.

She stayed that way for about three minutes then she lifted her head off of me and started kissing me on my neck and chest.

"Damn, this dick is good, Mandingo," she stammered. "Goddamn, this dick is good."

Before I knew what was happening, her mouth had found its way back down to my dick. She sucked it like I was about to give her a million dollars or something. Of course it didn't take long for me to get ready to bust.

When I felt it coming, I started pulling away. But she wouldn't let me.

"No!" she yelled. "I want to taste you this time. I don't want to waste a single drop."

I never told Karen Steinberg what I'm about to say. In fact, I've never told any woman what I learned that night. I found out that if you don't just try to go for yourself and actually keep the woman's enjoyment in mind then you will enjoy the sex just as much as she does, if not more. And she may let you get away with a few things she would have ordinarily freaked out about.

I can't believe she let me fuck her again after I came in her mouth. Then she let me come in her mouth again and swallowed it.

I have never been mad at Karen Steinberg since that day. Now, today, not only am I not mad at her but I love her. That's right—I love her. If you saw what I am seeing right now while Denise is undressing you would understand. I'm the luckiest man in the world right now because of a country-ass white girl named Karen Steinberg.

Like Don King says, "Only in America." Only in fucking America.

CHAPTER TWO

Denise Jackson

I've always loved my body but I became hyper aware of it the first time my mom's boyfriend had his way with me.

I was only thirteen at the time and an early bloomer. My mom cursed me out when I turned ten because she already had to buy me a training bra.

"I can tell that I'm gonna have problems with your fast ass," she used to say.

But I wasn't that big on boys. All I cared about was doing well in school so I wouldn't have to live the rest of my life poor the way I'd been living for as long as I remembered.

Anyway, my mom was working her dead-end job one night trying to collect overtime since her trifling-ass man had lost all of his money gambling again. Before she stomped out of the house, she told him that the least he could do was watch me when she went to work.

Up until that night, I had always loved how the rapist looked at me. My mom dressed me real corny-like every day in loose clothes that gave people the impression that I was either really fat or just funny shaped. No one ever saw that I was packing. Yet sometimes, when boys looked at me, I'd start singing the song Ed Lover and Dr. Dre made famous: "I'm naked underneath my clothes...I'm naked underneath my clothes."

I really didn't want to be with boys. But it was nice to get some attention every now and again. The only time I got attention at home was when the rapist chewed me up and spit me out with his eyes.

After my mom left, I went and put on my pink sweat-shorts. I used to stand in front of the mirror forever on Saturday mornings just to see how decent I looked in them. My ass was nice and plump and it always jiggled when I stood up on my toes.

If I could only wear some regular clothes, I'd be killing them in school, I used to say to myself.

I took my bra off and started rubbing on my breasts before I decided what shirt to wear. By then I was wearing a C cup, and I was mesmerized by how soft and perky they looked.

I pulled on a white undershirt and tied a knot in it just above my belly button. By then my nipples were hard and anyone would have been able to see my areolas through the thin white fabric. I wasn't wearing a bra.

Once I was convinced that the rapist would look at me the way I thought I needed him to at the time, I sashayed downstairs and commenced my performance.

I ran to the refrigerator and held it open while I was figuring out what to do next. I wasn't certain until the rapist chided me. Then I knew.

"You know what your mom say about holding dat 'frigerator open," he stammered.

Right on cue, I bent over and started fumbling around with some stuff on the bottom shelf. When he didn't continue protesting, I turned my head to see if he was watching me. Of course he was.

"Please don't tell my mom," I said innocently.

"You knows that I's ain't a tattle tale," he replied. "Plus, you and me can have secrets, right?"

Without answering, I just smiled and turned my head back towards the refrigerator, happy that I'd just gotten away with murder.

I felt good at that point but I wasn't satisfied. I got up and ran over to the sink and turned the water on really high. I can't tell you how many times my mom yelled at me in the rapist's presence about having the water on so high. But I was going for broke that night.

I grabbed a porcelain cup out of the dish rack even though my mom always demanded that I use plastic.

"My good cups are for company," she always said.

Nevertheless, I starting shaking the cup under the running water to rinse it out. Before long, I had made a mess. Water had splashed all over my shirt.

"Shit," I said, momentarily forgetting the rapist.

"What did you say, Denise?" he asked, sounding

stunned.

"I'm sorry," I said, turning toward him. "I won't say it anymore. Please don't tell my mom."

"'member what I said, girl," he replied. "Secrets."

I could barely hear what he was saying since his comments were directed to the titties that were jiggling around under my soaked white undershirt. If the rapist had ever wondered before, this time nothing was left to his imagination. When I looked down, I could tell as much, and for the first time, I wasn't happy to be stared at.

"Let me go change my shirt," I said.

"What for?" he asked. "It is kinda hot anyways. Cool yaself off."

"No. I think I'd better change it. My mom would kill me anyway."

"I told 'ya, secrets," he said.

By then, I was scared. I remember shrugging my shoulders and slowly walking to the refrigerator after turning off the water and putting down the cup. I never even looked in it again. I just closed the door and crept toward the entranceway of the kitchen.

"Where ya gon', girl?" he asked, grabbing my arm.

"I need to go upstairs," I said fearfully.

"No. Stay here with me," he demanded, his eyes ogling me and his hands gripping me tighter. In fact, he was holding me so tight I had a bruise on my arm for several days afterwards.

"But I have to change. I just have to change."

By that time I was crying. I can never remember what

he said to me after that. But what he did to me is forever etched in my mind, just as if it happened yesterday.

He grabbed at my breasts with one of his hands while holding me tight with his other. I cried violently and begged him to let go of me but he didn't. He continued to violate me by fondling me through my shirt until he finally just ripped it completely to shreds.

Once my naked breasts were revealed, he started sucking on them clumsily as if he was the thirteen-year-old virgin. At that point in my life I was clueless as to the right and wrong way to do what he was doing to me but I did know that he was hurting me. He was sucking on my titties so hard that my chest was purple, black and blue for close to two weeks after.

When he finally let go of my arm, the pain was so intense I couldn't even feel it anymore. I think it went numb. I started rubbing it to no avail until I had to use my hands to attempt to remove his hands from my ass.

Like a typical rapist, he had pulled himself really close to me so that I couldn't escape and palmed my ass through my favorite pink shorts with his nasty-ass hands. Before the night was over, he'd gotten so much filth on my shorts I never wore them again. Yet, at the time, I wasn't worried about my clothing. For good reason. I was worried about me.

I struggled with him meaninglessly as he pulled down my shorts. Once they were down, I regretted the fact that I hadn't pulled on a pair of panties. What I had always done to feel more comfortable was now just making things more convenient for the rapist. I was so frustrated with myself for being so stupid that I didn't know what to do.

When he started shoving his nasty hands up my virgin pride, I lost every ounce of fight.

"Stop. I'll let you do whatever you want but please wash your hands first," I begged him.

Surprisingly, he obliged by rushing over to the sink and washing his hands. Unfortunately, I was too shocked at that point to escape. I couldn't even scream. Hell, I didn't even whisper. I was stuck in a violent nightmare. Too bad I was wide awake.

I closed my eyes. It wasn't until he shoved his dripping wet fingers back inside of me that I realized that he was standing in front of me. He started kissing me all over with wet, sloppy, putrid kisses. If I'm remembering correctly, his breath made me throw up right in his face. But that didn't stop him. He was an old-ass fucking rapist who was overwhelmed with the idea of getting some young coochie. Not just any young coochie, though. He wanted my young coochie.

He took his belt off and unzipped his pants. When he pulled them down, I was appalled to see a shit streak running down the middle of his drawers. How could my mom stand to be with his filthy ass? His drawers practically stuck to his ass. I wouldn't have been surprised if some of his skin came off when he tugged his drawers down.

His was the first dick I had ever seen and it was the ugliest thing in the world. It was shriveled and old-looking. I didn't know it then but it was also little as shit. Well, thank God for small favors.

When his crusty little dick got his version of hard I knew there was no turning back. The rapist was about to have his way with me.

He turned me around and shoved himself inside of me without the slightest finesse or skill. Even though it didn't seem possible that his little-ass dick would hurt me, it did. I felt my hymen being ruptured. And when I looked down, specks of blood flecked my inner thighs. Not only did my arm and titties pulsate with pain, so did my girlish coochie. There was no question about it. I was definitely being raped.

I must have passed out but I don't remember for how long. But I do remember that upon hearing a familiar voice, I was jerked back to reality.

"What the fuck is going on here?" my mom screamed.

"Mommy! He's raping me," I cried through my tears.

"Rape my ass!" he shouted. "Dat li'l bitch wanted it."

"You little whore!" my mom snapped at me.

She rushed across the kitchen and started smacking the shit out of me. My face, neck, head, back. Every inch of my body stung by the time she finished with me.

"Get dressed and get the fuck out of here, you nasty bitch," she sneered. "You need to get away from me for the night before I kill your hot ass."

I was shocked, stunned, violated, in pain both mentally and physically, totally defeated. I threw on the first thing that I could find and dragged my weary body out of the house. But before slumping down against the tree that was just outside our shack, I heard my mom say words that have never left me.

"I can't believe her hot ass would accuse you of molesting her," she said. "That hot little bitch better recognize that I don't put shit before my man."

I could not believe that my mom would put that dirty, smelly, broke, little dick, old-ass man before me, her own daughter. Yet as surprised as I was at the choice she made that night, I was floored by the decision she made the next day.

When I woke up on the grass, a police officer standing over me. I didn't know what time it was but there was a hint of daylight.

"What are you doing out here, little girl?" he asked me. "Where are your parents?"

"My mom put me out the house last night because... because... because her boyfriend raped me and I told on him but she didn't believe me."

The cop looked me over carefully while trying to calm me down. By then I was crying hysterically.

Finally he asked, "Where do you live? I want to go straighten this out right now."

I was too upset to speak so I just pointed in the direction of our shack.

The cop grabbed my hand gently and walked me to our front door. He knocked repeatedly for about five minutes until we finally heard movement inside the house.

"Who the fuck is it at this time in the morning?" I

heard my mom yell through the door.

"It's the police, ma'am," he replied. "Open up. I believe I have your daughter out here."

I heard my mom unlock the deadbolt and unlatch the chain locks. The door swung open violently. My mom stood there on the other side, jacked up and irritated. After all these years, I can't forget how betrayed I felt knowing that my mom fucked the rapist the same night he violated me.

"Ma'am, are you alone?" the officer asked her.

"I'm in my own house, minding my own fucking business," she snapped. "You said you came to drop my daughter off and you did, so peace out. I ain't trying to fucking kick it with you."

"Actually, ma'am, I need to know if you are alone because from the looks of your daughter, I have probable cause to believe that something unsavory happened to her. If the suspect is here, I need to question him."

My mom shot me a look that could have cut diamonds.

"That's your ass if your bullshit causes any trouble," my mom snapped at me. "Do you hear me? That' your fucking ass!"

"Ma'am, do you see your daughter?" the cop asked her. "Her physical condition is consistent with her recollection of the events of last night. Don't you see her bruises, ma'am?"

"I already told you that I ain't' trying to kick it with you." She turned to me before continuing. "I told you that no trouble better come out of this."

My mom started to walk away but the cop immediately stopped her. "Ma'am, you need to relax," he said. "I need to be aware of your whereabouts at all times."

My mom shot back, "How the fuck do you expect me to get somebody if I can't move freely in my own damned house?"

"You can move freely," he said reassuringly. "But I have to accompany you."

"Fuck this!" she spat before calling up the stairs to the rapist. "Come here for a second," she said once he responded. Again, she shot me the nastiest glance she could muster.

As soon as the rapist's foot came off of the last step, the cop gripped him and cuffed him.

"Ma'am, if you'd like to come to the station you can follow us," the cop said, "I need both of them in order to run some tests. If you choose not to come, an officer will bring your daughter back home as soon as we finish with her."

"Let me fucking tell you something," my mom screamed. "Don't you fucking bring her ass back here! She done fucked around and got my man in trouble... don't you bring her fucking ass back here!"

My mom slammed the door with the force of an earthquake and never opened it up for me again. I'm not sure if she ever learned that the tests came back 100% conclusive that her man raped me. And God knows I don't know what happened to the rapist. All I'm sure about is that on that day an innocent thirteen year old grew up and began to fend for herself. I had to. I didn't have a choice.

I went through counseling for a little while after that and I know that I wasn't at fault for what happened. Yet I still blame myself. If I hadn't dressed so scantily in front of the rapist, maybe he wouldn't have been so tempted by me. Maybe everything would have been different.

But even though you can't change the past, the past can damn sure change you. That's why now, years later, I'm still funny about my body. Even in my line of work, I don't like people looking at me. In fact, I haven't been totally naked in front of anyone with the lights on since I was raped that day. Not until today. And even now, I'm crossing my arms, covering my breasts.

*****

"So, are we gonna do this?" Mandingo asks me. "Or have you changed your mind about putting me down with your program."

"I'm sorry, Mandingo," I said. "I was just haunted by a ghost from my past, that's all. I'm ready when you are."

Also coming soon...

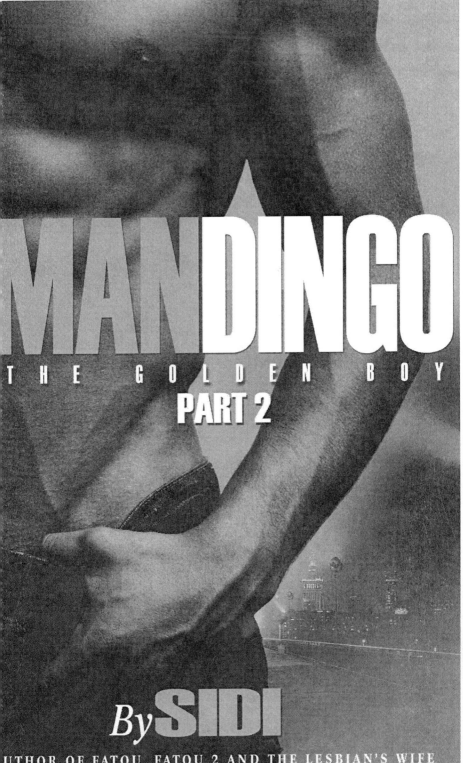

MANDINGO
THE GOLDEN BOY
PART 2

By SIDI

UTHOR OF FATOU, FATOU 2 AND THE LESBIAN'S WIFE

Mandingo:
The Golden Boy
Part 2

The golden boy, Mandingo, has warmed the beds of many women during New York City's chilly winter nights. Yet, since he didn't know or care about these women's marital status- many of them were married with children- eventually he finds himself in a world of trouble, facing deportation and even the threat of losing his life.

But, Mandingo isn't oblivious to the dangers ahead of him. After surviving a previous murder attempt, he told himself that he would be more careful. Yet, with so many women throwing themselves and their rich husbands' money at him, those words are easier said than done.

Mandingo received a blessing from God in the form of a new lease on life. But when his thirst for money, fame, and the mind control he has over the women he beds causes him to go fishing in a pond of women that are married to the most powerful and ruthless men in New York, will Mandingo open a can of worms that even he can't overcome?

Ride on Mandingo's wave of sex, money, and mayhem. Experience the chill of his manly prowess and the thrill of him trying to avoid the punishment that his enemies have in store for him. Then learn if Mandingo's over the top sex game can bring him the luck he needs to survive any and all pitfalls or if riding the dangerous wave of adulterous sex will finally make him wipe out once and for all.

the
Streets
of Harlem

BY LESTER MARROW

The Streets of Harlem

Lester Marrow grew up on the streets of Harlem during the drug epidemic that plagued the ghettos of New York City, and beyond, and defined the post-Vietnam War era. The Streets of Harlem is his real-life account of growing up in one of the roughest neighborhoods in the country.

In his matter-of-fact style, Lestoils (as many of his friends called him) tells the story of the drug game with brutal honesty and in graphic detail. He nostalgically recounts vicious childhood memories but flavors them with the bitterness of regret and resignation. His autobiography chronicles drug deals and near-arrests, murder sprees and sexual escapades, getting money and lots more money. And then losing it all to reckless drug addiction.

Throughout his life, Marrow's one constant love was music, and The Streets of Harlem is rich in the musical memories that accompanied many of his illegal and dangerous activities. Marrow was right there at the birth of hip hop and rap and tells how it all began.

The Streets of Harlem is truly a gripping story because it is REAL. Marrow's memories of his experiences will shock, terrify and frighten — and ultimately make you feel as if you lived those days right along with him.